UNDERGROUND

WOMEN

Also by Jesse Lee Kercheval

Fiction
The Alice Stories
Brazil
The Dogeater
The Museum of Happiness
My Life as a Silent Movie

Poetry
America that island off the coast of France
Chartreuse
Cinema Muto
Dog Angel
Extranjera / Stranger
Film History as Train Wreck
Torres / Towers
World as Dictionary

Nonfiction
Building Fiction: How to Develop Plot and Structure
Space: A Memoir

Translation
Fable of an Inconsolable Man
The Invisible Bridge / El puente invisible

Editor or coeditor
América invertida: An Anthology of Emerging Uruguayan Poets
Earth, Water and Sky: An Anthology of Environmental Poetry
Mis razones: Mujeres poetas del Uruguay
Trusting on the Wide Air

UNDERGROUND
WOMEN

Jesse Lee Kercheval

The University of Wisconsin Press

The University of Wisconsin Press
1930 Monroe Street, 3rd Floor
Madison, Wisconsin 53711-2059
uwpress.wisc.edu

Gray's Inn House, 127 Clerkenwell Road
London EC1R 5DB, United Kingdom
eurospanbookstore.com

Printed in the United States of America

This book may be available in a digital edition.

Library of Congress Cataloging-in-Publication Data
Names: Kercheval, Jesse Lee, author.
Title: Underground women / Jesse Lee Kercheval.
Description: Madison, Wisconsin: The University of Wisconsin Press, [2019]
| Includes stories from the author's 1987 book The Dogeater,
with the addition of three new stories and an afterword.
Identifiers: LCCN 2018046899 | ISBN 9780299323943 (pbk.: alk. paper)
Subjects: | LCGFT: Fiction. | Short stories.
Classification: LCC PS3561.E558 U53 2019 | DDC 813/.54—dc23
LC record available at https://lccn.loc.gov/2018046899

Eight of the stories included here appeared in *The Dogeater*, which was the winner of the
Associated Writing Programs Award in Short Fiction. Stories in this collection originally
appeared in the *Apalachee Quarterly, Carolina Quarterly, London Magazine, California
Quarterly, Intro 12, Ohio Review*, and the anthology *Micro Fiction*.

for

_____

Jerome Stern

Contents

UNDERGROUND

WOMEN

CARPATHIA

It happened on my parents' honeymoon. The fourth morning out from New York, Mother woke to find the *Carpathia* still, engines silent. She woke Father; they rushed to the deck in their nightgowns. The first thing they saw was the white of an ocean filled with ice, then they saw white boats, in groups of two or three, pulling slowly toward the *Carpathia*. My father read the name written in red across their bows—*Titanic*. The sun was shining. Here and there a deck chair floated on the calm sea. There was nothing else.

The survivors came on board in small groups. Women and children. Two sailors for each boat. The women of the *Carpathia* went to the women of the *Titanic*, wrapping them in their long warm furs. My mother left my father's side to go to them. The women went down on their knees on the deck and prayed, holding each other's children. My father stood looking at the icy water where, if he had been on the other ship, he would be.

When the *Carpathia* dropped off the survivors in New York, my parents too got off and took the train home, not talking much, the honeymoon anything but a success. At the welcome home party, my father got drunk. When someone asked about the *Titanic*, he said, "They should have put the men in the lifeboats. Men can marry again, have new families. What's the use of all those widows and orphans?" My mother, who was standing next to him, turned her face away. She was pregnant, eighteen. She was drowning. But there was no one to rescue her.

UNDERGROUND WOMEN

La photographie

I am taking a photograph of a Lavomatic near the Gare du Nord in Paris. It will be a color photograph that will show the walls sharp yellow, the machines the shiny white that means clean. The front of the Lavomatic is plate glass. Glass that lets out into the night the bright fluorescent light of the laundry. Glass that reflects a red hint of an ambulance beacon. Glass that lets the photographer catch this scene, this knot of official people grouped casually around a dark wrinkled shape on the floor. Catch at an angle of extreme foreshortening the stubby, already almost blue legs, the one out-flung hand holding one black sock. It will be the photograph of a dead woman.

Le Grand Hôtel

It is on the evening of my first day in Paris that I take the photograph of the dead woman in the Lavomatic and then check into Le Grand Hôtel de l'Univers Nord. At first I am tempted to find the name humorous—do the East, West, and South quarters of the universe keep separate grand hotels?—but decide against it. I do not know enough French to have any sense of humor in it at all.

Madame Desnos pleure

And it is the photograph of the Lavomatic or rather my memory of the dead woman in it that wakes me up so early at Le Grand Hôtel. I catch Madame Desnos, the *propriétaire*, in her leopard-spotted robe, still breaking the baguettes for the guests' breakfasts. "Mademoiselle . . ." she says, waving me to a seat at the counter. "His ankles," she remarks pleasantly, cracking off a six-inch hunk of bread. I think it is something colloquial and smile. "His knees," she adds, breaking off another piece, which I helpfully arrange in its basket. "My husband has sent me a postcard," Madame Desnos pauses to choose another loaf, "so he is not dead, and worse still, he says he misses me." She starts on a new loaf. "His spine." I drop a basket, and when I bend to pick it up, I see Madame Desnos's legs beneath her spotted robe. Like the woman in the Lavomatic, Madame Desnos's legs are protected only by hose fallen in wrinkled waves around her ankles, though hers are pink with only a foreshadowing of heavy blue veins. I begin to cry. Madame Desnos cries too, taking the scarf from her hair to wipe our tears. Her hair is the faded red of a very old dachshund.

"No, no, it's not so bad. I've paid off the loan he took out on the place the last time he came back." She pokes me in the navel with the last loaf of bread. "Smile," she says. "The mails are slow and people die every day." She breaks the bread in two. "His neck."

Le Grand Hôtel encore

After breakfast I become the desk clerk at Le Grand Hôtel. Perhaps in France people who want jobs as desk clerks always get up early and help with breakfast. "Remember," says Madame Desnos, "this arrondissement may be filled with hotels run by Algerians for Algerians, Vietnamese for Vietnamese, and Moroccans for Moroccans, but Le Grand Hôtel de l'Univers Nord is a French hotel," she waves a fine thin hand at the lobby, "that just happens to be filled with Algerians, Vietnamese, and Moroccans."

Monsieur Peret

I am polishing the big brass room keys the guests leave each morning when they go out to work or to look for work when a small man with very large false teeth appears suddenly at the door and rushes to kiss Madame Desnos on the cheek.

"Ah, Monsieur Peret," she says without looking up.

"Ah, ah, ah . . ." Monsieur Peret moans, "business is so bad, Madame, I have come to beg you to encourage your new clerk to mention the closeness of my excellent facilities to your guests." Monsieur Peret slides down the counter toward me and takes one end of the key I am polishing in his very tiny very clean hand. "Surely, Madame, you have already told your new clerk how much more reasonable my coin laundry is than that place over on the Rue de Ste. Marie, and how it is my standard and well-honored policy to offer one free wash with every three validated referrals? Surely, Madame, I need not mention these things myself." Monsieur Peret draws the key across the counter with my hand still attached. "Au revoir," he says, pecking me lightly with his dentures.

La photographie encore

I tell Madame Desnos about the photograph I took the night before of a dead woman in Monsieur Peret's Lavomatic, and she makes me go with her at once to the developer's. "It does not surprise me that a dead woman should bring Monsieur Peret's business trouble," says Madame Desnos as we wait for Monsieur Blanc, the developer, to bring out the prints. "Monsieur Peret was not good to his wife," she says, "and such things do not always go unpunished. He worked her so hard in that Lavomatic that to get some rest she went to a doctor and let him remove a part. Ah, but once the doctors start on someone they can never have done with them, and so they kept at poor Madame Peret until there was nothing left at all."

Monsieur Blanc brings out the dripping prints but Madame Desnos refuses to look at them until he leaves the room. She takes my hand, and I look again at the round dead shape of the woman in the Lavomatic.

"It's the way the customers are all just doing their wash, not even looking at her, that makes me want to cry," I tell Madame Desnos.

"Ah, but the only way a woman can make a mark on this world," says Madame Desnos, "is with her body. Surely not even a dead one should be allowed to go to waste. At least by dying in the Lavomatic she made a friend on the other side in Madame Peret." Madame Desnos puts the woman in the Lavomatic into a brown envelope for safekeeping. "Let us go see Monsieur Peret and let his complaining cheer us up."

Monsieur Peret encore

"Oh, she was not even a regular customer," Monsieur Peret complains before we are even inside the plate-glass wall of the Lavomatic. "And these people," he looks over his shoulder at the Moroccans and Algerians who are passing by outside in their dirty clothes, then waves a tiny clean hand at the empty laundry. "They are so superstitious. This picture on the wall," he takes Madame Desnos's sleeve and draws her to a small copy of a woodcut that is barely noticeable on the bright yellow wall. "It has been here for years—my poor wife picked it out the last time she was ever here—suddenly after this incident, over which I have no control, they complain about this picture. Just to cause me grief. There is nothing so irrational as a woman who has dirty laundry and wants an excuse not to do her wash." Monsieur Peret shakes his head. I move closer to examine the woodcut. It depicts five virgin martyrs being flayed.

Madame Desnos touches a long thin finger to one of the martyrs. "Perhaps if you feel you must replace this thoughtful gift of your wife's—would it not fit in somewhere in your own rooms?— the mademoiselle here could be of some service to you. I have just discovered she is a most accomplished photographer and plan to have some postal cards of the hotel made up expressly to utilize her talents."

"Well," Monsieur Peret looks from the flayed virgins to me, "perhaps a nice shot of myself, in a very white shirt, standing poised and attentive in front of the Lavomatic."

"Ah, well . . . perhaps the matter requires some thought," Madame Desnos says, "but I am certain if I talk to the mademoiselle we could all get what we deserve."

"Indeed," says Monsieur Peret.

Madame Desnos takes my arm as we leave. "We must think of something appropriate," she says to me.

Au cinéma

"Only every tenth movie shown in France can be made in America," Madame Desnos tells me as I am handing out the room keys to the returning guests. "And only every tenth song played on the radio. But," she says, "there are ways and there are ways: if a song is sung in French then it is a French song—no matter if it is 'The Yellow Rose of Texas.' So tonight we shall go to the movies and what we will see will be American movies so old they have become French by default."

After the last guest is in she tells the Algerians playing cards in the lobby where she will be in case the hotel catches fire or her husband returns, and we leave for the cinema.

"This theater has been running the same American serials since I was a bride," Madame Desnos tells me as we hurry to find our seats before the house lights go down. "I don't come here often, but slowly I am getting to see the beginning, middle, and end of them all."

We find our seats just in time. The lights go out. The titles come up on the screen: *The Queen of the Underground Women*. It stars Gene Autry as a radio station operator; under his Melody Ranch lives a kingdom of underground Amazons. After the titles the Queen of the Underground Women stands facing the camera and declares:

"Our lives are serene. Our minds are superior. Our achievements are greater than theirs. We must capture Gene Autry."

Madame Desnos pulls my arm and we get up and leave. Outside she shakes her head. "They are making a terrible mistake," she says.

Père Lachaise

After the keys are turned in the next morning, Madame Desnos announces we are going to make a small pilgrimage— "A pilgrimage is a trip that is its own reward," she says—to Père Lachaise, one of Paris's great cemeteries. On the way to the Métro she stops near the station and buys a stalk of hollyhocks. "For Madame Peret," she explains.

"Is Madame Peret buried at Père Lachaise then?" I ask. "No," says Madame Desnos, "there was so little left of her that Monsieur Peret let the doctors have that too, but it is a good place to be buried and a good place to visit the dead. We'll put the flowers on someone else's tomb, and, if it is important, perhaps they will tell Madame Peret we called."

In the Métro on the way to Pere Lachaise we sit in seats marked reserved in descending order for disabled veterans, the civil blind, civil amputees, pregnant women, and women with children in arms.

Madame Desnos shrugs. "So we are pregnant," she says, "that at least they don't make you carry papers to prove."

We walk from the Métro stop, through the gates of the cemetery, and then on over the crumbling hills of mausoleums, each family vault the size of an elevator, each with its shards of stained glass and leaf-clogged altar. There are cats everywhere, asleep under brown wreaths, fat and indifferent to the rain.

"Do you know," Madame Desnos asks, "that in Germany they only bury you for just a while—say until your husband remarries or your children move away. Then up you come, tombstone and all, and another German goes in your place. Busy people, the Germans."

We pass the tombs of Molière and La Fontaine, who are probably not really buried there, and the monument to the love of Heloise and Abelard, who most certainly are not, and then the grave of Colette, who is but hidden under her husband's name, and walk until we reach the columbarium with its tiered drawers of ashes.

"I am sure this is where Madame Peret would have chosen. She was a frugal woman, and there really wasn't much of her left." Madame Desnos runs one thin finger down a line of drawers. Names, dates, beloved this and thats—then she stops, her fingertip poised on a drawer with a black-and-white photograph of a young woman, a flapper, wearing only lipstick and long jet beads, a graceful hand poised beneath her chin and jet, jet eyes. No names, no dates.

Madame Desnos puts the hollyhocks in the flapper's dry urn.

Madame Desnos pleure encore

On the way back to Le Grand Hôtel we stop to shop at Printemps. Madame Desnos instructs me to buy a black bra.

"You American girls are not safe on the streets," she says to me and to the saleswoman in Lingerie. "Looking innocent is not protection." I remember Madame Peret's flayed virgins and think perhaps Madame Desnos has a point. We stop at a café for coffee and brandy to ward off the rain and then because of this must also stop across the street at an art nouveau underground toilette.

"Madame Desnos!" the attendant cries out when she comes down off the ladder where she has been fixing one of the tanks.

"Marie-Louise!" Madame Desnos squeals back, "I thought you were still in the Place St. Germaine."

"No, no I have been here for almost a month—a promotion."

"Indeed," says Madame Desnos, waving her long fine-fingered hand at the stained-glass lilies set in the stall doors, the hand-painted lily tiles, the murals of lily-languid young women.

I walk over and examine a beveled glass case behind the attendant's station. It is filled with little mementos of the sort nieces bring back to their favorite aunt. There is a stuffed baby alligator from Florida next to a set of Eiffel Tower salt and pepper shakers.

"Those were Madame Galfont's," Marie-Louise says, coming up behind me. "She was here for many years, since before the war, and had many regular clients."

"Madame Galfont has . . ." asks Madame Desnos with another wave of her hand, "passed on?"

"No, well, I usually say that she retired. It is a painful point." Marie-Louise shakes her head. "Did you see the signs on your way down the stairs?" She points up at some black and yellow government posters. "This new government—now they have boarded up all the pissoirs so the men too must pay a franc for a stall. Madame Galfont met a man in this way, and so she left . . ." Marie-Louise spreads her short arms in an encompassing gesture, ". . . this. I trained under Madame Galfont, to me it was as if she had abdicated." Marie-Louise shakes her head. Madame Desnos shakes her head. "So there was a meeting of all the attendants, all the women, and they voted that I should come here, and now I must be the one to show the new women how things have always been done, but I am no Madame Galfont." Marie-Louise takes a small Polaroid snapshot out of the beveled glass case. Madame Galfont smiles out of it, perhaps at some satisfied client, some tourist amazed at this splendid museum toilette. I look closer. I recognize Madame Galfont from another photograph, though in that one she is not smiling. I show Marie-Louise the woman in the Lavomatic. She cries. Madame Desnos cries. I cry.

Marie-Louise touches the printed image of Madame Galfont's outstretched hand. "A man's sock," she says and shakes her head one last time.

Marie-Louise takes the final picture of Madame Galfont and places it in the beveled case near the smiling Galfont, propping it up behind a pencil case from the Swiss Alps. The box cuts off the bottom of the picture—suddenly there is only the Lavomatic. White-coated officials view it with pride as busy customers concentrate on their wash. Madame Galfont is removed from the photograph as abruptly, as thoroughly, as she was from the Lavomatic itself, and yet . . . she is there. Gene Autry walking the hollow soil of his Melody Ranch, hurried Parisians whose footsteps I can hear on the sidewalk above—who cannot feel the presence of the Queen of the Underground Women? I turn to Madame Desnos.

"I have something for Monsieur Peret," I say.

La photographie encore une fois

I go back to Monsieur Blanc with the negative of the death of Madame Galfont.

"Cropped and blown up?" he asks.

"And framed," I say, "as large as possible and framed."

"Ah, well, for a friend of Monsieur Peret I think it can be arranged."

Monsieur Peret pour la dernière fois

Monsieur Peret straightens the framed photograph on the nail from which he has already exiled Madame Peret's virgin martyrs. "I am overcome," he says, still unable to decide once and for all that the picture is hanging level—he feels a certain unease about it. "Madame Desnos is too generous, too kind—a gift such as this . . ." Monsieur Peret stands lost in admiration for this magic-mirror copy of his Lavomatic and does not even notice two women behind him become nervous, take their laundry still damp from the dryers, and leave.

Madame Desnos ne pleure pas

When I return to Le Grand Hôtel I find a telegram lying open on the counter.

COMING HOME, BABY. STOP.

It is not signed, but I am sure Monsieur Desnos felt there would be no confusion. I go upstairs to pack. When I come back down with my bags, Madame Desnos's are standing in the hall.

"One moment!" she calls from behind the counter in the lobby. I watch as she takes each long brass room key and drops them one by one into her net shopping bag. We pick up our bags, and she locks the door of Le Grand Hôtel de l'Univers Nord behind us and puts that key too in her bag. We check our luggage at the Gare du Nord and then walk slowly toward the Seine.

"I have been in Paris a long time, but I was born in Troyes," says Madame Desnos as we draw even with Notre-Dame de Paris, Our Lady of Paris. "Troyes too has a cathedral, and in it the columns grow into trees, and the arched vaults are draped with grapevines. I think in Troyes they have done kinder things with their stone," she waves her fine hand at Notre-Dame's great east front, "than in Paris. In Troyes there are even carved escargot feeding among the marble vines."

We cross to the middle of the bridge from the Île de la Cité and stand looking back at the city.

"And in Troyes there is a woman who sits every day in the market and sells vegetables that the other vendors have thrown down on the floor as too old or too rotten. Yet from this woman even the mayor must wait in line each day and pay for the privilege of her weighing him out old parsnips." Madame Desnos unties her bag and reaches out the keys. "I think you would have to live in Troyes a long time to find out why this is so."

"Perhaps there are places where it is better for a woman to live."

Madame Desnos holds one of the brass keys between her long fine fingers and lets it drop into the Seine. I watch as one by one they fall, golden beads on a rosary, raising a tiny glinting splash apiece.

"Perhaps," Madame Desnos says, "perhaps."

A STORY SET IN GERMANY

I want to set a story in Germany—just set in Germany, not about Germany. Although my mother was German, I spent just a year there, winter to fall, and so know nothing about Germany but trivial things—that every window has lace curtains, that the phone system is the most expensive in the world, that I was often asked for directions by strangers when I too was lost.

So I will tell you the story that is set in Germany. The story as I wish it to be:

As a small train steams its way into the mountains an American girl on board is awed and struck by the dense German forests, by the dense German snow. She is going to live in a farmhouse high above the tiny town called the wild place, Wildflecken. Our American girl has a job teaching remedial English to the American soldiers at the post on the mountain opposite the mountain she will come to think of as her mountain, Ziegelhütte. The post plays no part in this story; pay no attention to it. Our American girl climbs up Ziegelhütte for the first time and meets her German landlords, Herr and Frau Fuss, who live alone on the mountain with only a tractor, three shaggy ponies—the Fusspferde—and a nervous wire-haired dachshund that Frau Fuss explains has *hundangst*—dog fear. Our American girl always calls the dachshund the Angsthund and so we will too. Frau Fuss is a huge healthy woman who, even in this heavily industrialized country, does much of the field work by hand. Herr Fuss is a dry stick of a man with emphysema so bad he cannot climb out of the potato cellar without resting, his wheezing kept company by the Angsthund's shrill yaps. Our American girl feels right at home because her mother was German, and after dinner each night sits and watches Frau Fuss knit. So the scene is set—it is lonely on the mountain, the Fusses are kind and parental, the wind is strong enough at night to knock a Fusspferd right off its hooves.

Enter the Jägermeister, the deer hunter, who drives a yellow Mercedes with matching yellow hubcaps. He rents the room next to our girl's and they must share a bathroom. He has known the Fusses for years, is a brewer from Würzburg renowned for the quality of his beer. He brings several cases for Herr Fuss in the trunk of the Mercedes. The Jägermeister is delighted to find our American girl there. He wants to work on his English, and so our girl checks out some books from the post library—which plays no more part in this story so don't bother imagining it—and the Jägermeister reads to her every night after dinner while Frau Fuss knits. He reads Dickens's *Bleak House* and does different clever accents for each of the characters. The crippled Phil Squad, who leaves a greasy track as he runs his bent head along the walls for support, is especially well done. One night after five-hundred pages or so, the Jägermeister puts his large warm hand over our girl's as he reads about spontaneous combustion.

The next day he takes our girl cross-country skiing on special skis he has made with sealskin-covered runners. The fur grabs the snow and they can walk up hills as well as slide down them. It is a trick he learned skiing in Norway. Frau Fuss has told her the Jägermeister goes out every day to feed the deer he will shoot in the fall. Instead he takes our girl out to help him move the hay bales and salt blocks the other hunters have left. He laughs at her surprise. It's no sport at all to shoot a pet deer, he says, and when they leave he erases their tracks with a fir branch.

When they get back to the farmhouse there is a note from Frau Fuss. She has gone with Herr Fuss to the hospital; he is very unwell. That night our American girl and the Jägermeister do not read Dickens. When Frau Fuss returns she says nothing, only sits alone with the Angsthund in her lap and works on the sweater she is knitting for him.

Some weeks later when the snow is beginning to melt and re-freeze into ice, a sure sign that spring is only a month or two away, our girl looks out the window and sees a Fusspferd run by kicking his shaggy heels in the snow. The Pferde have escaped. She runs after them, yelling to Frau Fuss who comes out of the house with her apron full of winter apples to coax the ponies, who are galloping jubilantly across the face of Ziegelhütte, back into their small paddock. The Jägermeister comes out too but laughs so hard at the sight of the Pferds, of stout Frau Fuss running after them, that he is no good at all. Our American girl is laughing too and keeps laughing when her feet hit a patch of ice and sail up over her head. When she lands and stops sliding, she stands and stops laughing— a little hurt. The Jägermeister puts her into the Mercedes, never minding the upholstery, and drives her to the post gates. She is taken from there to the post hospital—just imagine one room— olive drab. The Jägermeister is left standing by the guard house, a foreign national on this bit of German soil.

He sends her a set of Shakespeare's works in German. Only Germans share the English love of the bard, he writes in a note, because they have good translations, this one by Goethe. She lies bandaged in her army hospital bed and weeps at how beautiful the sonnets are in German. We do not need to know exactly what happened to our girl. No need to write a doctor into the story to carry the medical exposition. She bled and was bandaged and isn't scarred or deformed, only a little pale lying there on her iron army bed—whiter than her U.S. ARMY sheets, but they are a bit yellow. Every day our girl reads her Shakespeare and one day at the end of *As You Like It* she finds this note: *I must leave with the snow.* In German and in the back of a volume of Shakespeare this note is very touching and doesn't seem silly at all. Outside the sun is shining and the snow is almost gone, so our girl sneaks out of her olive drab room, waves to the gate guard as she passes him checking only the people who want to get in, and climbs gingerly up Ziegelhütte to find the Jägermeister just strapping his skis to the top of the yellow Mercedes. He weeps when he sees her and her things too are packed into the ample yellow trunk. Together they leave Ziegelhütte, with Frau Fuss waving and the Angsthund barking, and drive down through the mountains toward the brewery in Würzburg where the Jägermeister makes such good beer.

Later, when they hear Herr Fuss has died, they will send flowers.

So that is the story I wish to tell, the way I wish it had been, but it is not enough, is it?—this story only set in Germany. Since the war, Germany has not been easily allowed as a neutral background for stories, for lives. So I will try to give you a little more. Little by little I will try to tell you the little I know—that I only noticed as I was leaving how many patterns of lace curtains there were, the snowflakes, the sea shells, the delicate bent-necked cranes among delicate bent reeds, that as I was leaving I didn't use the most expensive phone system in the world to call and say good-bye to that gray-haired veteran of Hitler's army—the huntsman, the Jägermeister.

"Our American girl feels right at home because her mother was German."

My mother was a German war bride, but by the time I was born she was an American citizen. German was never spoken in our house unless my mother whispered it to me when I was asleep and safe from its charm. German food was not eaten in our house. My mother carefully followed the month's calendar of recipes that came in her *Woman's Day* magazine—tuna casserole made with Campbell's Cream of Celery Soup, meatloaf made with Lipton's Onion Soup Mix. Once when pork was a good buy and *Woman's Day* featured an Oktoberfest of German recipes—my mother carefully went back through September's calendar—Coca-Cola cake, Dream Whip waffles.

Once in the house of a grade school best friend I saw a picture over the sofa, a family portrait that had been folded into a dozen tiny squares, then unfolded and framed. Her family, my friend's mother explained to me. All of them died in the concentration camps during the war and only she escaped, carrying that picture folded in her shoe. I understood. My mother had pictures, too, of stiff-collared uncles and brothers and father, and high-haired dark-eyed aunts and sisters and mother. Hers all dead too, in the army, in the bombing, eating sugar beets in the rubble left after the war, but my mother's pictures were not framed on the wall but hidden in her underwear drawer beneath her heavy stitched bras. Because it wasn't the same thing, it wasn't at all.

As a child I always thought it was because of my father, this Americanization of my mother, but maybe not. Perhaps it was self-imposed, an act of contrition by a now-loyal ally. At my mother's funeral my dad turned to me, his hands shaking, his mind somewhere else, "You should learn German," he said. "It's a beautiful language." And so I did, in high school, in college. I did not show any inborn aptitude for it. Still that was no test, so I got a job in Germany, with Americans though, and went to find out how German I was.

"Our American girl has a job teaching remedial English to American soldiers."

The first thing I found out teaching Americans in Germany was that I did not really know anything about Americans at all. Once on a Greyhound bus back to college I'd been questioned by a German exchange student who'd just finished reading *Bury My Heart at Wounded Knee*. He wanted to know how recently I had oppressed a Native American—last week? last year? I had never seen a Native American. At the time I thought this encounter showed how little he knew about Americans, but really it shows how little either of us knew.

In my classes on the post I had Navahos and Hopis and Cherokees and Yavapais. And one-third of my students were native Spanish speakers, from Puerto Rico and Cuba and Texas and California. One low rider from L.A. told me how his mother and brother had been killed at the breakfast table by some kids who shot just for fun through the thin walls of his father's house. The boy cried as he said this, his lower lip pouting out where he had tattooed his mother's initials inside his lip. He couldn't wait to go back. He was going to sleep all day and then when his old lady got off work they would go riding, and it would be the best, the best life could offer. And Blacks, from bad Southern schools and bad Northern schools, most of them with their high school diplomas and still they couldn't read their MOS, their job manuals, and the army would bounce them out unless I could raise their reading test scores. And Samoans, from American Samoa. Huge men with names like Tulualualua, and one of them told me that at any given time half the men in Samoa were in the U.S. Army because there wasn't much else to do. Strangely enough the Samoans all liked Wildflecken, learned to ski, found its five months of winter fun for a change. The Germans I knew found it faintly depressing. So there I was in Germany teaching what was really English as a second language to American citizens. Compared to my students it was hard to work up a case for my not being a true American based on as small a flaw as having a mother who had been a citizen of the Reich.

"The post plays no part in this story."

Well, a small one. Hitler built it, not the Kaiser like most of the bases the Americans used, and our army used it as a live fire range and so it went on mile after classified mile beyond the solid stone buildings I saw, each with its own eagle over the door, its feet ragged where the swastika it once held had been chiseled away. From the range, if there was good snow to protect the German fields, would roll the American tanks out for a run between firing practices, and sometimes they rolled over not only fields but houses or cars. You have never seen anything quite as flat as a German car run over by an American tank. My soldiers swore it was a German trick, driving too close behind a tank so that the army would be forced to buy them a new car.

And in many ways the post was still a German post: Germans laid the beautiful patterned cobblestone roads, served the not-too-American food in the cafeteria, guarded the gates against unauthorized entry by young German terrorists. All this was done by old German men mostly, old enough to have been stationed there during the war, and on the gate one old man wore a death's head ring on his old hand. Its ruby eyes gleamed as he carefully checked my I.D. every day.

"Our American girl climbs Ziegelhütte for the first time and meets her German landlords, Herr and Frau Fuss."

And the Fusses too were old enough to have been there when the American troops rolled in the first time. All through the war the post on the mountain had stayed hidden by the thick firs and thick snow that our American girl would later admire. The Americans were down in the village, in Wildflecken, for a week before one of their patrols stumbled on the post, already evacuated. And the Fusses were there when it became a Displaced Persons Camp, and most of the firs were cut down for firewood by people just out of concentration camps who'd been sent into Wildflecken's long white winter, and there too when the DPs were replaced by waves of Germans coming in from the east, when the post that had once sat in the middle of Germany suddenly was looking down the Fulda Gap at the East German border, at Germans who were now the enemy.

But the Fusses are destined to remain flat characters, I fear. I do not know how they felt about any of these things. We never talked of them. Frau Fuss spoke a strong dialect of German and, although she smiled a great deal, I was never sure she understood what I said to her at all. Herr Fuss did not talk, only coughed and smoked, and did not read or write either. He would always wait until the beer man made his delivery to ask me for my rent, so the delivery man could write me a receipt.

The Fusspferde alone were revealed to me as not what they seemed, not stump-legged old ponies but rare Icelandic horses who belonged to a man who hoped the weather on Ziegelhütte was cold enough to breed them. It wasn't. In the winter they were happy but come spring they had to be shaved naked with the lambs.

And the old farmhouse was all alone on Ziegelhütte, but the isolation was somewhat broken by the *whumph-whumph-thud* of the big tank guns and the *brat-rat-rat* of the helicopters practicing their strafing. The windows rattled constantly but Frau Fuss said if one caulked them in tight they would crack or, if there was a big enough boom, explode.

"Enter the Jägermeister, the deer hunter."

His name was Karl Dietrich Rupert, and he had been staying at the Fusses for years, since his wife died, for vacations in the winter and fall, and he did have a yellow Mercedes with snow chains over its matching yellow hubcaps that he drove rather recklessly and used like a Land Rover, and he was a brewer from Würzburg, except that he was really a Berliner and so I suppose a DP, and he told me over and over that Berliners are the only Germans with a sense of humor, of proportion. He had not, though, been back to Berlin since the war. He spoke that lovely British English that is always a surprise to hear from the mouths of African presidents and Arab sheiks when they hold news conferences. He had learned it in a POW camp in Britain, a special camp, he will tell me later, for anti-fascist prisoners where everyone was given English language and history instruction—a lot about the Magna Carta and parliamentary democracy. He got in this special camp because his military record, captured along with his whole unit, said that he was to be watched, not to be entirely trusted. It said this on about half of the records of the men in his unit, he told me, and in his case it was because his wife had a half-brother who was a priest at the Vatican.

And so Herr Rupert wished to brush up on his English, which I found excellent, but which he decided was poor because when he spoke to the Puertoricaño soldiers down in Wildflecken they didn't seem to understand him. At his request I checked out some books from the base library which had a complete collection of the classics, which no one ever checked out. The only books that did a good business were the war books, ones with foldout maps of the Blitzkrieg, full color photos of S.S. regalia. Herr Rupert chose the Dickens. He was taught Dickens in school as a boy but had never read him in English. The library at the POW camp hadn't carried Dickens because his works criticized the English social system.

And so Herr Rupert read from Dickens every night, and he did do the most marvelous English characters—each one distinct. I can hear their voices still sometimes, and not always saying lines Dickens wrote for them. The characters in *Bleak House*, indeed all Dickens's characters, now for me always have a trace of a German accent as if they were continental cousins just in England for the holidays.

"One night after five hundred pages or so, the Jägermeister puts his large hand over our girl's as he reads about spontaneous combustion."

True enough, but let me tell you how I felt then. I wrapped my hand around one of his thick fingers and felt I was holding on to the most solid thing in the world, felt a warmth like I used to get when I was little from hugging my pillow as tight as I could. Even when I was at work, amazing my class by revealing that apostrophes are not random accent marks, I felt as if two huge warm hands were cupped around my heart. After he took my hand I couldn't help but call him Karl Dietrich.

And he did take me skiing on the special skis he'd learned to make in Norway during the war, and he did turn to me, a ten kilo block of salt on his shoulder, and say it wasn't sport to shoot a pet deer—but it did not stop at that. I couldn't help thinking about the German Jews, so warm and so safe and so sure they were Germans—hadn't that been like shooting pets? And even if I had asked Karl Dietrich and he said yes and so stood revealed as a man who is kind to animals and who regrets the sins of the past, he would also still have been a man who comes every year to shoot the deer he does not even feed in the winter—and so what would he have said if I had asked him about the gypsies, the Poles, the humans who had no right to expect kindness from the Reich who went to the camps? But you see, I couldn't ask. What did my mother think? Or if her being only a woman made her innocent, her father, her brothers? Did my mother marry an American to give her children the luxury of innocence? For the first time standing under those dark German firs I realized what it would have been like to grow up in Germany and to have had these thoughts all along. Or worse, never to have had them, the whole thing both too distant and too familiar to feel anything about at all. Once in fifth grade a girl had brought in some small snapshots for show and tell. Her father had taken them when the British liberated Bergen-Belsen. They were ordinary Brownie prints, out of focus, slightly yellowed. They were the most terrible things I had ever seen. When I first got to Germany the chief of the post photo shop said to me as he was making my I.D. that I should go to Dachau some weekend. The photos they have there in the reconstructed huts, in the museum, he said, are superb. Blown up to wall size and not a bit grainy.

"That night our American girl and the Jägermeister do not read Dickens."

Liebhaber, lover. I woke up the next morning thinking in German. That is at least part of the reason we gave up Dickens; I had to translate him in my mind to understand what Karl read. One of my Spanish students, who could speak English although he couldn't write it, said it always felt to him like it was coming from the right side of his brain—the spare room, as it were. My memories of this period seem a little distorted, the visuals seen from an odd angle. Maybe my student was on to the truth.

I remember one Sunday we drove in Karl's Mercedes over to the Kreuzberg, a mountain named after the cross the apostle of Germany placed at its crown, and sat drinking beer with the abbot of the monastery there—beer the monks have made for four hundred years. The abbot and Karl Dietrich talked brewing, their voices rising and falling, chanting almost, and I sat and watched the families drinking beer in the great hall that looked through a glass window at the huge copper vats. They would drink a few steins then go climb to the Calvary that marked the site of the saint's cross, then come back for more beer. It was touching and sincere and very different than my lukewarm Methodist upbringing had led me to expect from the Sunday choice between piety and sin. Half listening to the abbot and Karl, I caught in their malts and hops and bitters and strongs the shading and nuances of a sort of theology. Oh, if they had set out to discuss religion they would have used more conventional terminology, but it reminded me of a lay witness, an air conditioning repairman, I'd heard one slow Sunday in church. He compared searching for the will of God in the world to looking for a coolant leak that you know in your heart has to be there. A complete philosophy—what he knew as a metaphor for what he believed. It is a medieval concept, each small world the perfect reflection of the perfect whole, and it is a German concept. So I loved Karl because he could discuss beer as seriously as he would God, and I loved German because in it a discussion on hops could open a cold Sunday to the infinity of the universe.

"The Fusspferde have escaped."

They did and I fell and when I stood I felt a weight in my winter tights as if I had crouched in my bathing suit in shallow surf and scooped up a bottom full of sand. The snow turned red, melting a little, as my blood dripped down. Karl Dietrich held me in his arms while Frau Fuss ran into the house for a blanket to cover the car seat. On the way to the hospital my fear of bleeding to death was mingled with the knowledge I was ruining the seat covers in spite of this precaution.

"We do not need to know exactly what happened to our girl. No need to write a doctor into the story to carry the medical exposition."

But there was a doctor, a young major, who sat on the edge of my bed and took my hand. "Spontaneous abortion," he said.

I knew even without his explanation that what they had found in my stiff bloody tights was nothing, a dot of red flesh like you sometimes find in an egg you break open for breakfast. But whenever I think about it I see a pale tadpole of a baby, its wet underwater eyes open and startled, its wrinkled hands upraised, fingers curled, as if grabbing at space a second too late to catch hold. My German baby thrown out of my slick unnourishing American womb. Or worse, I see its eyes closed, its white hands raised palms out, like Jesus showing his wounds. A tiny German parachutist bailing out of my alien womb.

I woke up in my hospital bed thinking in English. Karl Dietrich sent me Goethe's Shakespeare and I couldn't even read the note that went with it. I think it was the baby who was fluent in German.

After two days when he didn't hear from me, Karl Dietrich sent me *Bleak House* with a marker clipped onto the page where we had stopped. I finished it. In the end Caddy Jellyby, a minor character who has been given a peek at happiness, has a baby born deaf and dumb, and her overworked husband's health is ruined. For the less interesting major characters all ends quite happily. Dickens buys belief in good with a dose of the unbearable. I hope that is not the way it works.

So I stayed in bed and in the hospital and safe on post and one day I woke to find the snow gone and I knew Karl Dietrich would be going too. And when I was better I went to Herr Fuss's funeral and took flowers. I put lots of blush on my cheeks and hugged

Frau Fuss hard so she could say to anyone who might ask that I seemed very well. At the end of *Bleak House*, I had found this:

Herr Karl Dietrich Rupert, Direktor
Würzburger Hofbrau Brauerei
Lindenstrasse 44
5500 Würzburg BRD

The Jägermeister's office address. And so I left. And even at the Frankfurt Airport with my pockets heavy with change that in nine hours would be useless, I did not call, did not use those phones so expensive yet so excellent that when he answered, my voice would sound so clear he would think I had come, was just down the street.

Waiting at the airport I did buy and drink a bottle of the Jägermeister's beer. I found it bitter—too much hops. But then my mother raised me on Wonder Bread and Velveeta and orange Kool-Aid, and when I think of home those are the foods that I crave.

WILLY

When Walt called at 6:30, I was drunk. He knew I would be, of course. Ever since he moved out, he times his communications with me for thirty minutes into the bourbon and after my 6 p.m. Valium. That way he doesn't have to worry about me asking any questions. Not that I questioned him when he said he had to have an apartment in the shadow of the Pentagon to be closer to his work—Walt is busy selling back to Defense all the knowledge they paid him to accumulate in his thirty years in the army. I knew the truth was that he couldn't face me the way I was, come home to a wife with problems after a day of solving ones with world consequences. But I didn't have the energy to try to make him say out loud that he was really leaving me, abandoning me—even if it was in a house whose bills he paid promptly and with a sense of duty.

"'lo, Helen," he'd say and then launch into the list of the expenses. That day when I heard him get as far as "forty gallons of heating oil," I put the phone down on the desk and let him talk to the philodendron while I went into the kitchen for some goldfish crackers. I got back in the middle of something different.

"Ted, after all these years—damn surprise. And him in consulting too." I started to put the phone back down, but I caught, ". . . kids fine, but Wilhelmina's in Walter Reed." Then I realized which Ted he was talking about. Wilhelmina's Ted. My Wilhelmina.

"In the hospital?" I said, startling Walt. "What's wrong? Is it serious? Is it cancer?"

"I didn't ask," he said.

How could you not ask, Walt?

Wilhelmina was my best friend when we were stationed in France together, in Fontainebleau just south of Paris in the golden pre–De Gaulle years. I had already been an army wife for ten years by then, but Willy was an outsider. To the wife part anyway.

She'd been a WAC major—the 41st WAC to go regular army, she told me. A WAC until she got pregnant and her Ted proposed with a gallant, "The C.O. says to make an honest woman out of you." One cold day when we were watching my Anna and her Johnny chase dead leaves in the Forest of Fontainebleau, Willy told me the army had offered her an abortion when she was pregnant. Willy shook her head, "I couldn't believe they'd break the law." That was Willy—her years in the army had given her great faith in rules. But THE RULES then said NO PREGNANT WACs, so Willy made her late entrance into my social world. Or I tried to convince her to. I took to Willy right away. Here was someone who could explain to me the military side of the army— all the things Walt was too busy to talk about. But Willy didn't try to mix with the other wives, play bridge, go to Hospital Circle meetings, join Refreshment Committees. I was hard on her for it at the time—I was like a high school girl, wanting all my friends to be popular. The army life stressed doing things in groups, was as strict as the nuns back in grammar school in its aversion for "particular friends." Group friendships were a protection against constant loss through transfer, retirement. Willy always thought such friendships were shallow—how could friends be as inter-changeable in the support they gave as bras? And it was true that no one really talked to anyone else, not like Willy and I did, but someone in the chain was always there—if you had to have a babysitter or got too drunk at the Officers' Club and needed to be taken to the ladies' room to lie down. But in all my army years, Wilhelmina was my one best friend. Maybe I shouldn't have allowed myself even one.

The Officers' Club Autumn Ball came along and that was too big a social event for even Willy to ignore. To get her excited about going, I had a dressmaker in Fontainebleau copy us gowns out of *Vogue*. I was too short for the season's square padded shoulders—my dress swallowed me up. But Willy looked smashing. Tall, blond, like Kate Hepburn mixed with Betty Grable. Then, the night of the ball, Walt told me Ted had gotten orders for Texas, and the fun went out of my plan.

Around ten—the invitations read eight, but only Walt believed it—the ballroom got crowded and hot. Willy grabbed my elbow and said she felt sick. We went into the garden. She sat down and put her head between her legs. "Oh, God," she said, "I think I'm pregnant again." We cried, Willy and I, out there in that damp French garden, hugging each other, crushing our new gowns. "Listen," Willy said at last, holding me at arm's length, "I don't want any Christmas cards with mimeographed newsletters in them. I don't want to send you a fruit cake and get it back 'Moved—No Forwarding Address.' We say good-bye first-rate friends, and when we meet up again, we start right where we left off. OK?" I must have said something back—OK, I guess—but all I remember is Willy's voice, tight, demanding, "No fade-out friendship—you hear me?" We sat on the stone bench, our arms around each other's padded shoulders, staring into the darkness as if our future was out there, waiting to run us down like a tank. When Willy left France, I was sure I would never see her again.

Then Walt, twenty years later, mentions her between the heating oil and the "Bye, Helen, gotta run"—with no idea what the news meant to me at all.

I called Walter Reed as soon as he hung up, but they wouldn't let me talk to Willy. "She's been medicated," a cool young voice said.

I went to see her the next morning, after my 10 a.m. Valium. I got the car carefully out of the garage at the time when, in the old days, I would have been at the commissary finding Walt something wonderful for dinner. It was a joke with us—how I'd found my way to his heart through his stomach. Every night after I told him what was for dessert, he'd say, "Strawberry shortcake—you can read me like a book," and kiss me on my temple, right where the blood leaves the head for the heart. But over the years dinner got quicker and quicker. He brought work home, then there were meetings to go to. You could see the nervousness in his eyes as he hurried even through dessert—afraid decisions were being made without him, maybe afraid they didn't really need him. Like a gambler who can't stand to be in the club room when the horses are running. So instead of grocery shopping, I drove carefully through D.C. where all the streets seemed to run one way the wrong direction. I finally asked a cop I'd circled three times how to get on Georgia Avenue, but after he told me, I missed the turn and went by him again. He raised his hands to heaven, "Jesus H. Christ!" his lips said.

Willy was down a very quiet hall. I thought this was a bad sign, being on a floor where no one was well enough to have *The Price Is Right* on loud. I was right to be worried. She looked godawful. I'd already double-checked the number on the door before I recognized Willy's eyes in the swollen lumpy face on the pillow. Willy's eyes, though, knew who I was at once. "Helen," she said, and didn't sound surprised. "God, don't look at me—I sure wouldn't want to. Turn on the TV, and we'll both look at that."

I stayed all day. Right through the game shows and into the soaps. She was still Willy. She complained about the way the WACs had been swallowed up by the army, women never training together, esprit de corps down the toilet. She mocked her civilian doctors—the army doesn't have enough doctors even to staff Walter Reed, its showcase, these days. How they weren't sure what she had in her, cancer, benign growth, just old rubbish. But fluid wasn't draining down through all the clever little valves and faucets in her liver. "Call Roto-Rooter that's the name," she sang, "and away go troubles down the drain." Just like Willy, but she got serious for a minute when *General Hospital* came on and the pale green room on the TV looked the same as hers.

She turned her eyes on me. "You don't look so good yourself, kiddo. You're not sick are you?"

"No, not really sick," I said. "I just don't feel well sometimes."

"Be well," she said, leaning out of her bed to put a swollen hand on my arm. "Once you give in to being sick, what happens isn't up to you anymore." She took her hand back and closed her eyes. "You get well and stay well. You hear me, Helen?"

"I will," I said. "Willy, I promise."

The nurse finally shooed me out when Willy's bowl of dinner came. When I got home, in spite of my promise, I felt so not well that I took two Valiums and got into the bourbon before the sun was over the yardarm, and still I shook as I lay on the couch watching Dan Rather. The phone rang promptly at 6:30, but I didn't answer it.

Why did you buy this house, Walt, if you weren't going to stay put?

Three years ago he bought this house, put me in it, and then ran back to his classified paper wars—where, as in any war, thoughts of family were put away for the duration, and men gave their all for the national defense. What was I supposed to do out here, in this suburb grown out of a cornfield, when he didn't even stay home to be fed breakfast and lunch? I had imagined the two of us flying around the world military space available, staying at Officers' Clubs in Calcutta and Nome. Or buying a Winnebago and having cactus fruit for dessert on the south rim of the Grand Canyon. I wanted us to be together. Instead I unpacked our green footlockers. Sent one of them off with Anna, packed with her *Playgirls* and her teddy bear, when she left to go to the University of Paris, to go back to France where she too had been happy. I put pictures on the walls for the first time in thirty years.

Walt had his consulting business to get going, and on the vast plain of civilian life there was nowhere to go and no one to go there with. There were no Wives' Bus Tours, no Officers' Club Bazaars. No one to come and sit with me and calm me down with endless hands of gin rummy and tiny tuna sandwiches. I couldn't relax. I paced from basement to attic and down again. I hung wallpaper. It wasn't straight. I took it down again. I cooked dinner for Walt and either burnt the food or burnt my fingers. I forgot to make dessert. I couldn't sleep and kept Walt awake when he had important meetings in the morning. He sent me to a doctor, a civilian specialist in internal medicine, whose waiting room was filled by women with vague interior complaints.

"Valium," a woman in his waiting room told me, "is what doctors give to women who cry in their offices, who take to their beds but can't sleep, who are in pain but aren't sick." The doctor prescribed 15mg ones for me.

Even then I couldn't relax. One day I walked out of the housing development—heeding the warning on the Valium label about handling heavy machinery—to the ABC Liquor a mile down the road. And I walked home again along the busy road with no sidewalk, ignoring the honking horns and startled looks, with a fifth of bourbon under my arm. At 5:00 I took a drink. At 5:15 I took another. Then I felt something give, something hard like the time I was chewing and my molar crumbled into dust. Then I relaxed. For two years.

I got to Walter Reed a little earlier the next morning. I'd only missed Georgia Avenue once this time, so I stopped in the gift shop and bought Art Buchwald's latest paperback. That would cheer Willy up. Buchwald had gotten his start writing on the International Herald-Tribune when we were in France, and Willy was a big fan. We'd even met him once, at a USO luncheon, although he was very shy and not at all funny in person.

I took the book upstairs with me, but Willy's room was empty. I thought I'd gotten the wrong floor and went all the way down in the elevator and retraced my steps. She still wasn't there. I sat down on the army-tight sheets of her vacant bed. I think I knew by then, but still, I decided I would wait. Surely they'd wheel her in any minute from one of the endless tests she'd joked about yesterday. I was thinking about turning on the TV when the nurse came in. She was pissed, of course, to find me wrinkling her sterile sheets, but I'm sure she thought she was being polite enough—they teach them that in nursing school. "You'll have to talk to her husband," she said. "He's already picked up her effects."

Oh, Willy.

Another nurse came in, a big black woman, who had taken her politeness course more to heart. "She died in her sleep, honey," she said, "not a bit of pain." Died medicated, she was really saying. With enough pills you don't even feel your own death.

Driving home everything seemed sharp enough to cut. Cracks in the road, starlings on phone lines—it was like Willy's death was an electric shock, jumpstarting nerves that hadn't worked in years. It was weird, and painful, but also as sweet and sour as a key lime pie. Suddenly I wanted to be alive even if it hurt like hell.

I pulled into the driveway and noticed for the first time that the house was the same puckery green as a cooking apple. I could taste it. I went straight upstairs to the kitchen, got down my refillable bottle of Valium, and dropped it down the garbage disposal. God, what a sound it made. The plastic screamed against the metal teeth. "There, Willy," I said, "well and getting weller." Then I got a lemon out of the refrigerator and stuffed it down after the pills. Nothing in this world smells lovelier than lemon rind down the garbage disposal. It made me cry to smell it. It made my head light. I left the kitchen to go down to the living room whistling, feeling buoyant as a party balloon. Then I fell down the stairs. I landed on my right shoulder, like a linebacker making a good tackle. Something went *crack-snap*, and there was such a stab of Valium-less pain I couldn't breathe. When I tried to stand, something went gently *pop* in my left hip, and I couldn't get up at all. "I'm not sick, Willy," I said lying there on the floor. "Just give me a minute."

At 6:30 the phone rang, and I thought, "Please, Walt, no answer two days in a row. Get worried. Come looking."

Instead a neighbor found me, Mrs. Pinter, a Korean war bride who was collecting for the Heart Fund but took me to the hospital instead. I had only dislocated my hip, but I had broken my collar bone, and that seemed to require that my entire upper body, including my right arm, be bound tight as a mummy. Mrs. Pinter waited for me, drove me home, tucked me into bed with the new pain pills that the doctor prescribed for me within easy reach on the night stand. She bowed politely before she left, refusing to consider my suggestion that she take whatever money was in my purse to help the hearts of America. I couldn't make it into the kitchen, so I flushed the pills down the toilet, then I lay back down on the bed and thought about dying. About lying there all wrapped up until I starved and dried up in my wrappings and turned into a real mummy. "Here I come, Willy," I said.

But I didn't. Quiet as cats the women of the neighborhood crept in. *Abandoned. Too sick to cook. Shouldn't be alone.* There, but for the grace of God, *go I, go I, go I.* They brought casseroles, congealed salads. The first couple of days I was too sick to eat what they brought. I threw up, and it seemed I could smell Valium in my urine, my sweat. Finally I managed to eat some congealed salad, holding it on my tongue until it dissolved. The women sat with me and told me where they'd come from and who they'd left behind, and I told them about Walt and about Willy.

A week after my accident, I was up, eating blintze and playing gin with Emma Rosen, a tiny Jewish woman who had lost every single member of her family in the concentration camps. She cried, and I held her hand as she showed me the official lists that traced her dead down through second cousins, then the phone rang, and it was Walt. He had just read the *Post*, he said, and first he called Ted, then me. Wilhelmina's funeral was today, 4:00 at Arlington. She had passed away last Wednesday, but there was an autopsy, and Arlington wouldn't schedule until the body was released. "I'm sorry, Helen," he said. "Should I come and get you?"

It would take Walt an hour from the Pentagon then maybe more going back as rush hour started. Mrs. Rosen held out her watch—it was almost 2:30. "No," I said, "I can get to Arlington. Will you be there?"

"I'll try," Walt said.

I ransacked the closets for something black to wear to the funeral and found a wool skirt that was probably Anna's, but with my arm lashed down none of my blouses would fit. Mrs. Rosen took me across the street to Mrs. Gjerde's house—she of the congealed salad—and I borrowed a black tent top from the very back of her closet. "My size 16 wardrobe," she explained, "for right after Christmas."

"Can you drive?" I asked Mrs. Gjerde. She shook her head. I told Walt I'd get there. I looked at Mrs. Rosen. Her face flushed.

"They took my license away," she said.

"Well," I said, "you can work the turn signal."

I couldn't turn around to back the car out, but luckily I'd left it in the middle of the double-car garage. And luckily, to Walt a car wasn't a car without an automatic transmission and power steering. Still, every pothole brought unmuffled pain. Tears came out of my eyes and dried where I could taste them. But my mind was as clear as the pain, and I pulled into Arlington at 3:30 without having gotten lost once.

Walt was waiting on the steps of the reception building. A girl in a blue blazer with an American flag on the pocket tried to take my arm, but I waved her away. She took Mrs. Rosen's instead and led her inside.

I walked up to Walt.

"You're hurt," he said. He didn't seem surprised—maybe the neighborhood women had been talking to him too.

"A war wound," I said. Walt considered me and nodded, almost with respect. I considered him and thought he looked as bad as I did.

"You're all right then?" he asked.

"Almost," I said, "and you?"

"I've never been so tired."

"We're not young."

"No."

I started up the stairs, wanting to go in together on this note of agreement, but Walt stopped me. "I can't stay—a meeting," he said, but with no excitement in his voice. Sounding as tired as he looked.

"That's all right."

"No," Walt said, "it's not."

"No," I said, and we stood, in agreement for a second time. I waved him down the stairs. "Come by the house," I said. "We'll talk."

Ted was in the waiting room talking to Mrs. Rosen. I almost didn't recognize him in civilian clothes.

"I had to pull strings," he was explaining, "to get my wife into Arlington. These days it's for field-ranking officers only, full colonel and up." Mrs. Rosen nodded. "Hell, I'm a lieutenant colonel, and I don't even qualify." He made a face. "But Wil's being the 41st WAC cut the mustard with this woman general I got hold of. That's the army," he shrugged, "an exception for every rule."

And since he'd gotten Willy in, I knew that Ted would also be an exception to the rule. A man has a right to be buried with his wife, and Willy's body was holding Ted's place.

Ted saw me in the door and stood up. He didn't recognize me, so I reminded him, and he looked nervous. Afraid, I think, that I might do something awkward like cry.

A woman wearing a corsage of mums with petals like white cockatoo feathers came in and introduced herself as the Defense Department Representative. Then the girl in the blue blazer shooed us out into waiting limousines. Ted got in one with the woman from Defense, and Mrs. Rosen and I got in the other.

It was a splendid funeral, Willy.

Full Military Honors. A company of Old Guards from Fort Myers, all six feet tall, formed the honor guard, and there was a marching band, complete with tuba. Four gray horses pulled the caisson with Willy's flag-draped coffin, and behind it was a tall black horse with an empty saddle. A mount for the fallen rider, for Wilhelmina.

The woman soldier who was our driver said the horse was Black Jack Pershing, and this was his last funeral before being retired to Virginia. "Black Jack followed President John Kennedy to his grave," she said.

We rolled slowly through Arlington, to a measured drumbeat from the band. On the reviewing stand in front of the Veterans' Day Memorial, a hundred or so tourists watched us, the last full honors funeral of the day. They were wearing shorts, sneakers, instamatics, but they stood as Black Jack passed, quiet and respectful.

Willy's grave was on the flat land near the Potomac, not up on one of the green hills, but it was a nice site, close to a small tulip tree. The four of us sat in folding chairs facing a patch of Astroturf that covered the open grave, and Mrs. Rosen began to cry softly. The chaplain gave a short eulogy based on Willy's military record. "Honorably discharged," he concluded, "Wilhelmina went on to send two sons into military service. John is serving on the USS *Lexington*, and his brother, Victor, is stationed in Turkey." Until then I hadn't known Willy's French pregnancy had given her another son. Then the honor guard folded the flag from Willy's coffin, snapping it crisply, and the chaplain presented it to Ted. "For your wife's service to her country," he said. The band started playing something low and sad, like a hymn but with a touch of military march; the seven soldiers in the honor guard fired three volleys with their rifles, aiming toward the Pentagon. A soldier lifted the Astroturf, and four Old Guards lowered Willy slowly into the grave. The soldier laid the green carpet back over her. Mrs. Rosen cried harder.

Then the woman from Defense stood up. The band started playing something snappy. Ted stood. The honor guard formed in ranks on the road. Mrs. Rosen stood. The band marched off, the horses starting after them. Mrs. Rosen raised her hands toward Willy, then to the sky, and began to moan. Her voice starting low, hoarse, then rising. The woman from Defense turned toward her, even her cockatoo corsage looking startled. Mrs. Rosen went down on her knees on the Astroturf. Ted turned away. Mrs. Rosen moaned louder, shaking her head from side to side. And then I moaned too, feeling something moving deep under my bandages. Not even the army can make partings painless. To feel loss, to grieve—this is a promise we make when we love. I would feel this for Walt, or he for me. It was inevitable. And it made him precious, Willy precious.

"Willy, Willy, my friend," I was crying, "I'll miss you, I'll miss you." Black Jack screamed, his bridle rattling as he shook his head, but Mrs. Rosen's voice rose higher even than that. Our sorrow rising into the air above Arlington, above the Potomac, up to meet the jets taking off from Bowling Green, from Andrews, up to the very boundaries of the national defense.

CIVIL SERVICE

I am a G.S. 13, a federal civil servant, a bureaucrat. I am Janet Marie Nedermacher. I have been Janet Nedermacher at least since I learned to spell such an intricate name in Miss Miggleton's primary class. I have been a G.S. 13 only since this last September.

I took the Federal Civil Service Examination on September 15th; after a lifetime of taking tests it was routine for me, not even a peak performance. I got the results on the twenty-first. I did well. Not for me the filing of a lowly G.S. 5 or 6, G.S. 13 is a rank the government bestows with unsuperstitious pride.

When I walked into the Federal Bureau of Personnel to post my scores I walked away from twenty-five years as a student. I remembered what Monsieur Plaichard, my plump communist French instructor, had been so fond of saying, "Parochial schools breed nuns and government schools petty bureaucrats."

On September 24th I was formally classified as an Administrative Trainee, assigned to the Treasury Department, Check Claims Division, in the old Liberty Loan Building. *Old* is the key word here. It is a World War I temporary building. Franklin Delano Roosevelt saw in these never-torn-down buildings proof of the relentless expansion of government. When World War II made more temporary buildings a necessary evil F.D.R. was moved to say, "This time I want the damn things built so they fall down ten minutes after the armistice is signed."

43

Poor Franklin, the government that won't tear down a building won't let one fall down either. It is an axiom of the civil service that the only thing worse than a WWI temp is a WWII temp and the only thing worse than a WWII temp is the fifth circle of hell.

Liberty Loan is a great wooden drum of a building that smells mysteriously of cat piss and Xerox machines. I was struck by this strange odor the first day I trudged up the four slick flights to Check Claims. It was accentuated by a terrible fetid heat. I later learned that the steam heat was ritually fired up on the tenth of September and everyone kept fans on high and windows wide to combat this artificial return of August's misery.

Check Claims occupies an L-shaped room that is half of the fourth floor. It is an uninterrupted expanse of metal desks bounded on one side by a dark wall of files and on the other by uncurtained windows. The walls are two-tone green, rather like an old Chevrolet. The linoleum, black-on-white, has worn gray-on-gray along the major thoroughfares. At the elbow of the room there is a glassed-in office which, like a widow's walk, commands a relentless view. Stiff black letters on the door read,

SUPERVISOR
CHECK CLAIMS DIVISION
MARGARET ST. CLAIRE

On that first morning I clutched my personnel forms to my breast as I clicked up the gray linoleum path and into that glass cell. Supervisor St. Claire did not look up. She continued scratching away at a memo with a fountain pen. The girl in Personnel had warned me, "As far as I know St. Claire came with the building."

If so, she wore it well. Her face was unmarked except for thin creases that ran parallel to her long fine nose. Her hair was pressed in a firm gray helmet that brooked no compromise with fashion. She wore a navy dress with white linen cuffs and collar clasped at the throat by a cameo of Diana hunting. I can't seem to recall her ever wearing anything else, though she must have changed.

I announced my presence.

She looked up, carefully set down her pen, folded her long hands. I felt a sincere and not altogether unreligious desire to genuflect.

She nodded twice.

"Welcome to Check Claims, Miss Nedermacher. I've asked Mr. Jenks, our custodian, to bring in a desk for you. I'm afraid it will be a bit crowded but I'm sure you won't be with us long." She cut off my budding protest with a firm nod. "Just standard procedure with Trainees, onward, onward."

"Christian Soldiers," I thought.

"Mr. Rosen will show you our Trainee arrangements. If you have any questions don't hesitate to file an interoffice memo. Please close the door on your way out, Miss Nedermacher."

I was back outside before you could nod twice.

The office was, my father would have said, a regular cat house. All women, mean age about sixty. The florescent lights gleamed off rows of silvered heads. One lady's hair glowed a relentless blue. The desks were covered with ceramic pots of philodendrons and pictures of grandchildren on tricycles.

"Ms. Nidermacher?" The deep voice made me flinch.

"Man in the Hall!" I thought, startled back to my days in the girls' dorm. "Nedermacher," I corrected and turned to face the voice. It belonged to a man about twenty-eight with sad brown eyes set over a long nose. He looked like a dachshund. Dachshunds are my favorite breed of dog.

"Haven't you a first name?" he demanded. "Nederwhatever is quite beyond me."

"Janet."

"I'm Carl, Carl Rosen. Come on, let's get away from the Crystal Palace," he said, glancing back at the Supervisor's office.

We went to a huddle of desks in the far end of the L by the windows. "This is the Playpen."

"Oh, Carl," protested a dark girl with brittle red nails. "Stop teasing." She turned to me, "This is where the Trainee's desks are."

"Janet, this is Maria and vice versa," Carl ventured gallantly. Maria and I nodded at one another.

"Maria Dressler," she added.

"Well dearheart, any questions?" Carl asked.

"What, exactly," I said, "do we do around here?"

"Nothing," said Maria.

"And more nothing," added Carl.

"Unless you want to grind through those." Maria waved a crimson-tipped finger at a green metal bookcase piled high with ragged, bound copies of government regulations. Dusty, yellow, I could see one titled "Interstate Pulp and Lumber Regulations of 1932."

"Supervisor St. Claire doesn't approve of Trainees," Carl said. "We're just outsiders to her, almost as bad as civilians. She doesn't trust us with any work. If you sit real still and be real quiet she'll sign your transfer and you'll be out and into a real job. If you don't, well a letter of reprimand could keep you here until the Washington Monument is worn down to a nub."

"You're going to be here until you retire, Carl." Maria frowned.

"Ah, just an anarchist at heart." Carl grinned at me. "So, Princess what do you think so far?"

"I think I would like to find my desk." I took the middle ground.

"Noncommittal, eh? We'll draw you into our madness yet, just you wait and see." He trotted off in search of Mr. Jenks and my desk.

Carl was right. I tried to resist, but boredom wore me down, and I found myself drifting into the waiting arms of the rebel camp.

From October 2nd through the 6th I sat at my desk, except for trips to the metal bookcase, and read a vast quantity of government memorabilia. None of the regulations books appeared to have any relation to the functions of the Treasury Department. None of them mentioned Check Claims. I remained diligent, I was rewarded with a sinus headache, filthy hands, and several nasty paper cuts.

On October 6th I sent a memo to Supervisor St. Claire asking for an outline of my duties. I got back a memo with the single word *Observe* written and underlined in india ink.

From the sixth to the ninth I sat and observed. On October 10th I observed Carl lead the Trainees out to lunch at the tavern across the street at eleven and they did not come back until one. I ate a baloney sandwich at my desk.

On October 11th this popular tactic was repeated. I weakened and went out with them but came back punctually at twelve.

Carl bought me a beer.

On October 13th Carl set our clock ahead. We all trooped off to our weekends, past the astonished faces of the regulars, an hour early.

Carl took me to dinner. On October 20th we started a perpetual poker game. This proved a nice supplement to my income but we lost Helen O'Day. She went straight and begged for a transfer after losing everything but her virginity in a marathon session.

After seven years of college, I was back at summer camp.

Carl remained hardcore. He said he was sure if he was obnoxious enough the Sup. would transfer him to save us. Personally, I thought it likely to be a long war and prepared to find comfort in the trenches.

I asked Carl to my place for dinner.

The rest of the office, what Carl always called the regulars or Mother Margeret's gray ladies, seemed very busy. The fountain pens scratched from eight till five. Everyone in the office wrote out their cases in longhand with fountain pens. There was not one typewriter or Government Property Do Not Remove ballpoint in the entire place.

On October 31st Supervisor St. Claire sent for me. I went heart and hat in hand.

"I have been too busy to give you much personal attention, Miss Nedermacher. I regret that sincerely and apologize," she began, nodding emphasis. Her eyes were tight and tired. "I have been examining your personnel file and I am most impressed. You are a G.S. 13. I, Miss Nedermacher, am also a 13."

Her confession touched me. I nodded.

"I am of the opinion that any further extension of your training period would be a waste of my time and yours."

"Sweet Holy Jesus," I thought, "my transfer out of Check Claims."

"You have been assigned to the position of Assistant Supervisor, Check Claims. Mr. Jenks will move your desk. Congratulations, Miss Nedermacher. I am sure that you are pleased with your promotion as well as proud of this opportunity to serve Check Claims in a formal and permanent capacity." She nodded and smiled warmly. "Please close the door on your way out."

November began and my life fell apart. Traitor, collaborator, I followed my desk across the room and became a man without a country. No explanations would suffice. These things are based on instinct.

I was not welcome on long lunches. No amount of money could buy me into the poker game. Carl was never going to go to bed with me. But busy hands make a happy heart. I set out to find the true meaning of Check Claims. I had status now. I went around and demanded to review people's cases and was gratified with instant results and detailed explanations.

It seemed simple. Everyone thinks he is entitled to a government check and nearly everyone is, sometime. These checks are issued. Some are variously stolen, lost, forged, spindled, or mutilated. Some checks are issued fraudulently. The resulting letters, anguished pleas, or irate complaints end up in Check Claims.

Take the case of one Roy Cornet, a store owner in Rowan County, Kentucky. For thirty years he cashed a monthly government disability check for Mrs. Rita Plunkett. The checks were issued to one Ira Plunkett, Rita's lawful husband. On the first of every month for thirty years Mr. Cornet would ask Mrs. Plunkett, "How's Ira doing?"

"His legs are knotted up terrible, Roy," or "He's a mite better today. Sittin' up," Mrs. Plunkett would reply, take the $261 and return to the hills.

It came to the attention of the Treasury Department that for twenty-five of those thirty years, Ira Plunkett had been neither better nor worse but altogether dead. Roy Cornet cashed the checks improperly, ergo, he owes the government $78,000 plus interest. Mrs. Plunkett died and thus escaped effective prosecution. She didn't leave any of the money behind.

On the whole I found Check Claims less demanding than poker.

On November 10th, I got up early and lay in wait for Supervisor St. Claire at the elevator. Only administrators were allowed to use the one elevator in the building. It was an ancient freight elevator that only Mr. Jenks, the custodian, could coax into motion. He ran it solely for Margeret St. Clair. Anyone else who wished to use it had to hunt Jenks down and offer him bribes. For Miss Margeret he waited, pulley motors warm and clanking, at seven every morning. From November 10th on I joined them every day and split their morning ritual into an unhappy threesome. It meant getting up an hour earlier, but now that my nights were empty, it made little difference.

On November 30th the first flurries of snow fell. In the face of need the heat cut off. The Trainees went home. The regulars just put on their coats. I stayed and put on my parka and mittens. We moved our desks closer together and Margeret St. Claire sent out for hot chocolate.

On December 3rd the heat came back on and the sudden dryness gave me a violent nosebleed. Viola Retner, the lady whose blue hair I had noticed the first day, took me to the ladies lounge and packed ice against the back of my neck.

In the next week I began to notice how all the little extra tasks in the office fell to Viola. People sent her for paper clips and coffee. She always took up the collections for gifts and flowers. She dusted what the janitor ignored. She did all these things gladly and everyone seemed to assume she had no better work to do. This seemed oddly humble. Viola Retner was a G.S. 9. Sensitive now to the hierarchy of these things, it seemed improper that 5s or 7s should take her servitude for granted.

Yet in a way I could understand. Viola radiated maternal comfort that begged to be of personal service. She had a plump pillowed body, soft with scented talc. She often wore the color violet. Her fountain pen was filled with not black but peacock blue ink, rather the color of her hair. She wrote memos on scented stationery with violets across the top. She began to bring me tea every morning, since I don't drink coffee. She would stand by my desk responding to my tales of woe with gentle clicks of her tongue.

I was curious about her work, she spent so little time at her desk. I reviewed her files of cases. They were filled with letters started then never finished, with wrong forms incorrectly filled in. A case would sit on Viola's cluttered desk for a month or two, then she would date it and print on the outside of the manila folder in peacock blue ink, Review in Six Months. I felt sick in the face of such sweet incompetence. I stopped drinking tea.

On December 15th I did what I never thought I would do, I turned to Margeret St. Claire and dumped the whole thing on her.

CIVIL SERVICE

"Janet," she said and her head shook in an involuntary parody of her usual nod. "Will you trust me on this and believe me when I say the situation is one only I can handle?" She plucked nervously at her cameo. I realized she was afraid of me. Afraid of me and of the Trainees. She thought us filled with the bitterness of ungrateful children. And I thought perhaps she was right.

"Viola has been with us a long time," she continued, "and she deserves our consideration. Her retirement, her pension could be at stake here. Do you understand what that would mean?"

Freeze frame: kindly old lady goes over the hill to the poorhouse. Violet living on Medicare and cat tuna. I understood in that instant how little of my civil servant's soul belonged to those distant taxpayers.

"I understand completely, I wouldn't go over your head on this. It's strictly intraoffice." I heard myself saying.

"Thank you for your discretion in this matter. I'm pleased with your concern for the welfare of Check Claims." She was in control again. She nodded and smiled as I left.

The next morning I was ten minutes late and Margeret St. Claire had Jenks hold the elevator for me.

On December 20th I spent an entire lunch hour caught up in a discussion of Jello recipes with Mrs. Custerman, who wears an over-the-counter hearing aid. I shouted myself hoarse and felt myself skidding toward the edge.

I decided to take my two weeks annual leave alongside the Christmas holidays.

On December 23th I sat through the office Christmas party. I was waiting to pick up my check, which regulations state is not available before 3:30, even though accounting had printed them up the day before and were now all downstairs partying.

Carl, Maria, and the other Trainees were on a different pay cycle and they didn't bother to come in that day at all.

The Christmas party was an office tradition. All of the gray ladies brought covered dishes. Mrs. Custerman brought a peach

Jello. Someone spiked the ginger ale punch. Everyone began to giggle and sing carols in unsteady soprano tones. There were presents under a tiny plastic tree. Viola handed them out. She gave me three. I felt ashamed. I had cared so little for these people, knew them not at all, and yet they had thought of me and felt me one of them. Observe. There is none so blind as she who keeps her fists screwed up over her eyes.

I opened my gifts.

The entire office, collection taken up by Viola no doubt, gave me a set of silver fountain pens.

Viola gave me a box of violet scented talc.

The third gift was from Margeret St. Claire. As I opened it she got up and went to stir the punch. In the box lay the intricate antique cameo, Diana pointing straight at me. The delicate surface shone dreamily under the harsh florescent lights.

"I so rarely wear jewelry," Margeret St. Claire murmured.

The punch seemed to settle in my knees. I sat down heavily and began to cry.

Viola and the tiny pigeon-toed Mrs. Grimshaw helped me into my parka. Viola stood in the hall with me while someone went for Mr. Jenks.

"I'll just take the stairs," I remember repeating. "Nothing to it, do it all the time."

Mr. Jenks prepared the elevator for descent. Viola pressed close to me. She squeezed my hand.

"Please, Janet," she whispered, "don't worry about my cases any more. I'm such a poor silly old fool and everyone watches out for me. Margeret gives me cases that are already closed. She thinks I don't know. Please don't think so badly of me, I do the best I can."

I think I hugged her. The elevator went down.

I sat across the street in my car for a long time. I rolled down the windows and let the bitter December wind blow through. I pinned on the cameo brooch.

I thought I saw, in the still-lit windows of the office above, two figures watching. A tall shadow bent protectively over a short plump one.

On January 15th I came home from vacation with a Florida tan and a relaxed mind. I came home to bad weather and brutal news.

On January 3rd Viola Retner had entered Sisters of Mercy Hospital to have a small lump out of her breast. That night, before a surgeon could lay a knife on her billowing softness, her heart stopped. An autopsy showed the tumor to be benign.

Still in Florida, I missed the funeral. Everyone else in the office had gone, though no one remembered to take up a collection for flowers.

On January 6th it had started sleeting and Margeret St. Claire called in sick.

So when I returned to work on the 15th, I returned as Acting Supervisor, Check Claims Division.

On January 23rd Margeret St. Claire finally came in to work. She moved with measured difficulty, her skin drawn painfully tight. Our eyes followed her, pleading security. She stopped in front of her office and spoke with Mrs. Custerman. She picked up a pen and began to jot a note. She dropped the pad. She stared at the pen. Slowly she unscrewed the cartridge. Peacock Blue ink spilled down her long fingers and spread bright and terrible across her white cuffs. Over in the Trainees corner Maria Dressler let out an hysterical squeak.

"Margeret," Mrs. Custerman began. Margeret St. Claire set the pen down, oh so carefully, turned her back on us and walked out. I heard the stairs creak as she went down them.

On February 1st the District police found Margeret St. Claire standing alone in a freezing rain waiting patiently on a corner where no buses had stopped in twenty years, a transit token in her open hand. Supplication, she stood, her arms outstretched. The quality of mercy is not strained. It droppeth as the gentle rain from heaven.

She was taken to Colombia General and sent straight to intensive care. On February 2nd I went to see her. I told a young intern she was my great-aunt and he signed me in.

"Pneumonia is often an old person's best friend," the doctor assured me.

Margeret St. Claire did not agree. Her eyes burned with words the tubes would not permit her lips. Needles ran into fine veins that shone against white skin with an all-too-familiar shade of blue.

The funeral was on Sunday. On Monday I rode the elevator in lonely splendor. I spent most of the morning cleaning out Margeret's desk. Scented notes in peacock blue ink.

I threw them away unread.

I ordered Mr. Jenks to change the name on the door. I told Carl he was going out to dinner with me and shut him up by sending him down to Supply with a requisition for three cartons of black ballpoint pens. Maria Dressler went into hysterics. I spoke to her sternly, threatened to dock her a day's pay for conduct unbecoming a government employee, then sent her home on paid sick leave.

The King is Dead, Long Live the King. I rode the elevator down at five. I met Carl as he came down the stairs.

From the office of
Janet Marie Nedermacher
Supervisor
Check Claims Division

A CLEAN HOUSE

When Harriet Gundy broke her back, she was making up the bed in the guest bedroom of the apartment where she had lived for fifty-two years—since the Alhambra Arms had been built along with Country Club Plaza and the planned Moorish part of Kansas City. No one had slept in the guest bedroom all fall, but Harriet thought the sheets might be musty. She was just lifting the corner of the mattress a little to tuck the corners under—how many thousands of times had she done that?—when something inside her gave way. Crumbled, like the time one of her molars turned to dust in her mouth. Then there was pain, not just in a tooth this time, but everywhere, in every nerve.

At St. Luke's the doctor told her she didn't have enough calcium in her bones. He called it osteoporosis and showed her X-rays in which her vertebrae, her ribs, were just ghosts, barely visible. "It's a common complaint in older women," he said. "Especially," seeing her daughter Bobbi's age on the chart, "in women who have children late in life." The fetus had priority over the mother when it came to calcium and took it where it could find it—from the mother's teeth, bones.

It was a disturbing idea, but on the whole Harriet couldn't think of anyone she would rather have given her calcium to than Bobbi. At least it had gone for something. She'd had Bobbi and

Bobbi had gone on to have Jason and Laura and now had (as they said when Harriet was young) a bun in the oven—five months into the creation of another little being.

After her doctor left, Harriet called Bobbi. The hospital operator said getting to call Wiesbaden, West Germany, where Bobbi's husband was an Air Force dentist, was the most exciting thing she'd done all day. But Harriet didn't tell Bobbi she was in the hospital. She listened to Bobbi's voice saying this and that about her husband's plans for starting in private practice as soon as his tour of duty was up and about Jason's and Laura's progress through nursery school, kindergarten. She listened behind Bobbi's voice and heard the children yelling half-heartedly at each other. She heard a TV and a washing machine.

"I just read an article," Harriet said to Bobbi, "about how important calcium is." From across the ocean she heard Bobbi's washing machine begin its spin cycle. "I really just called to make sure you were getting enough calcium."

"Oh, Mother," Bobbi said, "calcium, potassium, iron—you should see the list of things I have to take. It's all so scientific now. I don't know which is longer—the list of things I have to eat or the list of things I can't."

It turned out there wasn't much the hospital could do about her broken back. Her doctor said there wasn't any point in putting her in a cast—it would only weaken her muscle tone. It wasn't like there was a fracture, he said, with bone sticking out this way and that. Two vertebrae that had been there just weren't there anymore. Some nerves were being pinched, but, if she would lie still for a while, those nerves would die. Then the rest of her back could go on like before. She would just be a little shorter.

Except, Harriet realized, it could happen again. She wondered if a person could live without any bones at all and found herself imagining between breakfast and lunch that she was a jellyfish floating between the white hospital sheets.

After two weeks, her doctor let her go home. It amazed her how dirty her apartment had gotten in fourteen empty days. There was dust on the mahogany coffee table. Dust on the shelves and shelves of books her husband had collected, rescued from decay, from basements, from people's laziness in the nick of time. Even though he had been dead eleven years, she felt ashamed. Dust rose from the Persian carpet as she crossed the living room, and she heard a soft rustling coming from the books—like cockroaches eating the glue from the bindings. Ashamed.

In the kitchen the coffee cup she had used the morning she broke her back had gray mold growing up its white sides. How many times had she washed that cup? Dusted those books? She opened the refrigerator. There was sweet bad air in it. Under the Saran Wrap things were growing on leftover pot roast. She opened the vegetable crisper. A bright, waxy orange glowed up at her, looking the same as it had the day it arrived with eleven others—a gift from an old neighbor now in Florida. She bent to pick it up but her fingers went through the orange's skin and into its wet, rotten center. The bottom was bright green with mold.

She stood at the sink and let water run over her hand. Ten stories below her kitchen window, she could see Brush Creek running in its concrete bed. Two years ago she'd looked out the window and seen it way over its banks, running gray and ugly through the Plaza, through Saks, Neiman-Marcus. Standing at her kitchen window she'd seen a dark spot in the gray of the stream that looked like a person hanging on to a lamppost. She left the window to call the police (the number was busy), and when she came back the spot was gone. The paper the next morning said people had been swept from cars in the parking garage.

Now standing with her hand under the water, still smelling the rotten orange, Harriet thought she understood the limits of how long a person could hold on. She felt on the edge of despair. She looked at her mother's silver coffee service sitting tarnished on the buffet, at the dark gilt-framed oil paintings of Venice that she had bought on her honeymoon grand tour of Europe. Except for two days in St. Luke's when Bobbi was born, she had cleaned this apartment every day for fifty-two years, and it still needed to be done all over again. She picked up her dirty coffee cup and—even though it was one of an Irish bone china set of eight that Bobbi fully expected to inherit—threw it in the trash.

Her doctor, since he was a gerontologist, knew a lot about old people even though he was young. "When you get older," he had told her, "you can't do what you used to do." He had given her the number of a county agency that matched live-in help, nursing students, practical nurses, with people who needed helping. She called the number, and they said they would send someone as soon as they could. The only hired help she'd had was a big woman her husband had gotten to help in the last uncomfortable days before she went into labor with Bobbi. Every morning the woman burned a whole pound of bacon, and then, when it returned from the breakfast table untouched, ate it all herself. Even now when Harriet smelled bacon frying she thought of how swollen, how nauseated she had been.

The agency sent a skinny white girl, Jean Knowles. She wore a white turtleneck and a pair of pale blue jeans that had been thoroughly ironed. She had short blond hair still a little damp from its latest shampoo and blue eyes only a shade darker than her jeans. She sat at the opposite end of the kitchen table from Harriet, with her hands—whose nails looked as soft as if fresh from a sink of dishwater—folded on the tablecloth in front of her. She was the cleanest, most scrubbed and bleached-looking person Harriet had ever seen.

"I've completed the first year of my A.S. in nursing, Mrs. Gundy," Jean said. Her voice, her face, as relaxed and clean of expression as her folded hands.

"You've decided to take this fall off?"

"The dean of the nursing school suggested it," Jean said, with no hint in her voice how she felt about the suggestion.

Jean handed her a note from the woman at the agency. Harriet held it for a moment, looking over at Jean, wondering how she could tell her she just wouldn't do, tell the woman at the agency to send someone lively and fat who wouldn't make the apartment look twice as dirty by contrast, make her feel ashamed of how disordered her apartment, her life had become. But the note said that after careful consideration of Harriet's needs, Jean was the only candidate the agency could put forward at this time.

Jean looked politely out the window at the Plaza while Harriet considered the note. "Well, dear, I guess you'll want to move a few things in," she said. Jean turned her eyes from the window to Harriet. Her face was still relaxed, without expression really, but Harriet felt as if Jean were smiling at her.

When Jean returned that afternoon with one small suitcase, Harriet offered her the guest bedroom with its cherry dresser and bed, its Martha Washington bedspread. But Jean took Bobbi's old room instead, even though Bobbi had taken all her childhood furniture into her marriage, leaving nothing in the room but a single bed and a lamp. Jean cleaned her new room, the floor, the walls with buckets of hot water and some cleaner that smelled like lemon. She put fresh white sheets on her bed.

That night Jean made a dinner of two lightly broiled chicken breasts, two fresh fruit salads, and two tall glasses of iced tea. The table looked like summer, so light, so sunny. Harriet had never eaten a meal quite like it, though she had seen pictures of such food on the covers of magazines at the supermarket checkout counter. Just looking at Jean's food made Harriet think all the meals she'd prepared in the same kitchen had been the wrong kind, too heavy, too fatty. Just the kind of cooking to spread grease out beyond the exhaust fan to cloud the windows, darken the wallpaper. Jean had put a thin slice of lemon in each tall tea glass. The chicken tasted faintly of lemon as well. It reminded Harriet of one afternoon tea with a long-dead great aunt. Harriet had put first the cream she was offered and then the lemon in her tea. The cream curdled instantly. Since then, she realized, she'd stuck to cream, to butter, to richness. But sitting with Jean drinking lemon tea and breathing air fresh with lemon cleaner she felt, even though it was a gray fall night, that there was sunlight in the room.

Mondays and Fridays, Harriet spent all day at St. Luke's having calcium dripped through an IV tube into her arm. Or so her doctor said—the bottles the nurses hooked up to her seemed to be filled with clear water. When she wheeled her IV stand into the bathroom, that's what seemed to come out as well. On these days Jean would drop her off at the clinic then go back to the apartment to clean. When Jean brought her home from her first Monday spent at the clinic, Harriet felt right away that the apartment was different—more than just cleaner, actually lighter, bigger. It took her several minutes to realize all the bookshelves in the living room were empty.

"I put them in your storage room in the basement, Mrs. Gundy," Jean said. "The superintendent helped me get them boxed and in the freight elevator. There was no way I could clean them. If you want a book to read I'll go down and get it for you—I labeled the boxes." But Harriet couldn't think of one title Jean must have magic-markered on the boxes. It suddenly seemed strange to her to have spent all those mornings dusting books she never read. Jean hadn't replaced the books with bric-a-brac. The shelves were wiped very clean, and the empty square spaces made the living room much larger, as if each were a mirror reflecting a clean, empty room.

"Silver tarnishes," Jean said Friday morning before taking Harriet to the clinic. She picked up the coffee service on its heavy scrolled tray. "Wouldn't this be better in a safety deposit box?"

In Jean's clean hands the silver service looked useless to Harriet. Had she or her mother before her ever poured coffee from that pot? How could she ask Jean to waste precious time the way she had polishing what wouldn't stay clean? "Put it in the storage room," she told her. She couldn't imagine anyone wanting to steal such a useless thing.

After that, every Monday and Friday, Harriet returned to find something had vanished down the freight elevator. Sometimes it took Harriet quite a while to figure out what was missing. Strange how she could hardly remember pictures, lamps, vases, things she had looked at for years, once they were out of her sight. Each thing, no matter how small in itself, left the apartment a little larger, lighter.

The only room Jean left undisturbed was Harriet's bedroom. Harriet couldn't imagine her dresser without the silver framed snapshots of her grandchildren, of Bobbi. The walls without the wedding portraits of her father and mother, herself and her husband, Bobbi and her dentist in uniform.

"Don't bother straightening up in here," Harriet told Jean. "It's such a muddle. Just make up the bed."

But rather than resting in her bed, Harriet spent whole days on the living room couch that Jean had covered with white sheets. For years she had rarely gone into the room except to straighten the pictures, the magazines on the coffee table. Now on the bare coffee table she and Jean played dominoes—the white and black tiles cool in her hand. They played in the afternoons when she wasn't at the clinic. After a while they didn't keep score.

One Friday in late October, Harriet came back from the clinic and asked to see the storeroom. She'd been thinking about one painting that used to hang in the hall—had it been a clown or a ballerina? Something cheerful like that. As soon as Jean unlocked the door she knew she shouldn't have asked. It was like a room full of corpses. Every object in the room had been decaying for years—right under her eyes, while she dusted without seeing what she dusted. All her dusting hadn't kept the picture—a small girl dressed like a ballerina—from fading, hadn't stopped time. Memories, as well as dust, clung to everything. Some were surprisingly painful—the pierced brass lamp her husband had had his secretary pick out for an anniversary present that suited the secretary much more than Harriet. And even the pleasant memories—a glass Siamese cat Bobbi had given her one Mother's Day—were sad because they made Harriet regret having lived past such moments, made her want to go back and hide in some chosen safe hour. She stepped back from the door. Jean closed and locked it.

The next Friday at the clinic one of the nurses helped her out of bed and broke four of Harriet's ribs. She had to stay in St. Luke's to make sure no bit of bone had managed, even in its softened state, to puncture her lung. She had trouble keeping down the hospital food, and more X-rays showed a small ulcer. The nurses came by every four hours with little paper cups full of Maalox, but still she hardly had any appetite.

After a week, her doctor let Jean come to take her home. As soon as Harriet stepped into the apartment, she knew how busy Jean's week had been. The carpets had been taken up, and oak floors Harriet had forgotten gleamed with wax. The wallpaper in the kitchen and bathroom had been stripped and the walls painted with white enamel. The brocade curtains were gone from the windows in the living room, and there was nothing but clean glass between the room and the sky. After all, Harriet thought, what do we have to hide? She lay on the couch and felt the apartment around her like a nearly invisible container—like the glass bottle that held the clear liquid they ran through her body at the clinic. I feel, she thought, like water in a glass.

After her stomach trouble started, Harriet noticed that Jean always ate exactly the same amount of food she did. She hadn't noticed before because Jean fixed equal portions and both of them had cleaned their plates. But now, when Jean fixed two small filets of sole, two lemon custards, Harriet couldn't eat half of what was on her plate. Jean left the very same things. Harriet watched her. She would carefully cut her fish into squares, but she would never take a bite until Harriet had. If Harriet took one bite of custard, Jean did. If Harriet left hers untouched, then a perfect pair of custards went down the garbage disposal.

This was true of everything Harriet ate or drank except her morning coffee. She still insisted on a cup in the morning, though it was on her doctor's long list of things-your-ulcer-won't-like. Jean would pour herself a cup and sit at the kitchen table with Harriet, but she only held it to her lips now and then. The cup never got any emptier.

"Is it too hot for you, dear?" Harriet asked.

"Hot?" Jean put her fingertips against the coffeepot that she'd taken perking from the stove a moment before. She held them there. Her face, as usual, was free of any particular expression. "Yes, I guess it is hot," she said at last and moved her hand. Harriet could see that the ends of her fingers were red, a blister rising already on her pinkie, but Jean stirred her coffee and didn't seem to feel any pain at all. She'd taken Jean for granted, Harriet thought. Seen the services, but not the servant. Jean, more than the apartment, was the glass holding her life. Jean had taken away her other worries, but now, Harriet realized, she had Jean to worry about.

Her doctor decided the trips to St. Luke's were too hard for her. Besides, in spite of the gallons of calcium-rich water poured through her body, her bones weren't any darker on the X-rays. So she and Jean played dominoes every afternoon. One day, when they stopped for Jean to fix dinner, Harriet looked out the window and saw red and green lights come on, outlining all the stores in the Plaza. Somehow she had missed Thanksgiving. It was time to start shopping for Christmas. She had always loved Christmas shopping, especially for Bobbi, for Jason and Laura. She was famous for finding just the right thing, for giving each person at least one object of their heart's desire. She asked Jean to take her shopping.

Jean checked out a wheelchair from the Plaza office. It was crowded—Harriet could never remember it being so crowded. She decided to get the children's presents first. "Christmas," she shouted to Jean over the noise, "is really for children." So they went up in the elevator to the toy department. It was chaos. Jean got her out of the elevator, but then they were stuck, pinned between a model-train layout with Santa riding in the caboose and a table covered with mechanical dogs. The dogs hopped blindly back and forth on the table, falling over, bumping into each other, and at the downbeat of every hop they barked. Not together, because some had fresh batteries and others had been hopping and barking too long to endure. Jean managed to edge the wheelchair away from the train set, but one footrest jammed against the dog table. The dogs hopped up and down right under Harriet's nose. The dog closest to her hopped very haltingly, his bark so run down it was like a moan, like soft crying.

"Please," Harriet said, waving her hand at him, "I can't stand it." Jean leaned over her and picked up the toy. There was a pink plastic switch in its stomach.

"No need to be sad, Mrs. Gundy," Jean said, her finger on the switch. "See," she pushed it over. "It goes—then it stops. On—Off. It's a robot," Jean set it on the table. "A robot just like me."

Harriet let it go until dinner. They had left the Plaza without buying anything at all. Harriet was so tired she fell asleep in the car during the two-block ride home. She dreamed of lifting up Jean's shirt and finding a hard plastic switch where her belly button should be.

Harriet waited until Jean had cut up her veal into identical bites, then she asked, "Why did you say you were a robot?"

Jean looked at her with the look Harriet sometimes felt was a smile. "Because I am. That's what it said in the note the woman from the agency sent you—wasn't it?"

"No," Harriet said, "it wasn't. Besides it's not the sort of thing I would just take someone's word for."

Jean set her fork down. "Look," she said. She reached up and plucked gently at her eye with her thumb and index finger—just like Bobbi had finally learned to do with her contact lenses. And Jean held out on her fingertip a tiny round bit of plastic like one of Bobbi's lenses—but she did it with such seriousness that Harriet was afraid to look up, to look into her eye, for fear there wouldn't be anything but wires and glowing tubes. She looked. Jean's eye was still there, pale blue, a little watery from being poked at. "See," Jean said, and put her contact back in with a single easy motion. And then Harriet knew Jean was mad. She knew it in the same instant she realized she loved her.

"If you're a robot," Harriet said, "why do you have to eat?"

"I don't digest food," Jean said. "I only eat to encourage you to eat." She waved a hand at Harriet's plate, a very thin, white, little hand. Harriet realized for the first time how much weight Jean had lost eating only as much as an invalid old woman and yet cleaning, cleaning so hard. She ate looking at Jean, ate every bite on the plate.

Harriet didn't know what to do. She thought about calling the woman at the agency—but how could she tell a stranger about Jean's problem? What would become of her? What would become of Harriet without her? In the end she called Bobbi—not to tell her about Jean but to tell her she would be sending checks to the children this year instead of presents. A gentle hint to Bobbi that her mother was aging, might soon need all her daughter's attention. But when Bobbi answered the phone, Harriet almost hung up. It was something in Bobbi's voice. Even though she sounded pleased, under that happy tone was a hint of all her others. Her teenage grumpiness that had lasted ten years. Her newlywed begging—you don't need that, do you?—when can I have that, Mother?—that had seemed at the time to count Harriet already in her grave. It wasn't that Bobbi wasn't a sweet girl, a good girl, but the sound of her voice made Harriet feel swollen and awful as if the last slow days of her pregnancy had never come to an end, as if she were still carrying Bobbi, growing heavy, heavier, under her skin.

Harriet managed to tell Bobbi about her decision not to buy presents. "Jason and Laura are old enough to pick out their own toys. I don't know what kids want these days—all these fads." Bobbi was more upset than Harriet thought she would be.

"What's really the matter, Mother? Are you sick? Have you been to a doctor?"

She went on, but Harriet could hardly hear her for a terrible popping and buzzing that had come on the line. "Do you hear that awful noise?" she asked.

"What, Mom? Oh, it's not the connection. I was just frying some bacon."

Harriet thought for a moment she would faint or be sick. Bacon. She could smell it as clearly as if she really was still pregnant.

"Mom, are you still there? I turned off the burner. Mom?"

Harriet hung up. Jean came to her from the kitchen. She took a wet cloth and sponged Harriet's forehead. She laid her down on the couch and gave her a cool alcohol bath. She wiped Harriet's hand once, then again, until Harriet no longer smelled cooking fat or felt sick at her stomach. Smelled nothing but the evaporating alcohol.

Four days later, Harriet was resting on the couch, feeling tired. There was a soft pressure in her chest. Jean thought it might be a cold, so when the doorbell rang she was in the kitchen squeezing fresh orange juice. She went to answer the door with a dry empty skin in one hand. It was Bobbi. Harriet couldn't focus on her she moved into the living room so quickly, pregnant stomach first. She spun around on her heels, taking in the changes in the apartment she'd grown up in. Harriet saw her mouth open but then instead of words coming through the air to Harriet's ears, time stopped. Pain stopped it. A tearing pain that dug its sharp heels into her chest, then ran hard up her left arm. She couldn't breathe. She thought, though she couldn't feel it, that she was crying. She could see only a tiny tunnel of light, but framed in it she saw Jean's white hand pushing at Bobbi's back, pushing her out of sight into the darkness.

"I love you," she called out to Bobbi leaving her, to Jean barely still there.

At St. Luke's her doctor spread her electrocardiogram out on her bed like a comforter and said it showed her heart and arteries were as hard as her bones were soft. It was a shame, Harriet thought, she'd gotten used to the idea of being a jellyfish and something in her went and got rigid again.

Her doctor wouldn't let her have any visitors, but she could see shadows standing sometimes beyond the curtained glass wall of the cardiac unit. She imagined her doctor telling Bobbi that old people just couldn't do everything they used to—stretching it to cover not talking to their own daughters. After a few days, she got a pad from a nurse and wrote Bobbi a note.

> Give my love to Jason and Laura and to your baby when it's born. Please get Jean to give you the key to the storage room. All the things there are yours. I can't care for things the way I used to. So please take the things you remember and the love you remember and go home to your children.
>
> Much love,
> Mother

She sent the nurse out to the shadows with the note.

The next morning she woke to find the curtain drawn back and Jean and Bobbi standing beyond the glass, talking. Bobbi turned, as if she felt her mother's eyes. She raised a hand, half waving, half pleading—just like she had leaving for the first day of kindergarten. Harriet smiled and nodded as she had done then—go, go, the whole world is waiting. Then Bobbi was gone, and after a few minutes a nurse brought Jean in. She sat down quietly.

"I promised Bobbi I would call," she said, "if anything happens."

"You mean if I die?" Harriet asked.

"If you die," Jean said, touching a finger to Harriet's hand below her IV.

This time Harriet wasn't sure how many days passed before Jean came to take her home. Jean looked very thin, as if she hadn't eaten at all while Harriet was gone. As usual, Jean had been busy. She had cleaned Harriet's bedroom. But on the new white walls she had hung four old pictures—a baby Bobbi, baby Jason, baby Laura, and one Harriet almost didn't recognize, herself as a baby. In place of the old mahogany poster bed stood a white hospital bed whose head could be raised and lowered with the touch of a switch. A robot bed, Harriet thought, as she settled between the white covers.

They both napped. The afternoon sun shone through the window on Harriet in her new bed and on Jean in the chair beside her. Her head rested on the edge of Harriet's pillow. When the sun went down, Jean fixed dinner. Two bowls of golden chicken broth. Two cups of hot tea with tiny curls of fresh lemon. Then she sat again in the chair. Both of them rested for a moment, only looking at the bowls of soup on the tray. Jean straightened Harriet's pillows and, with a push of a white button, raised the head of the bed. Harriet looked at Jean and felt warm tears start down her cheeks.

"Did I hurt you, Mrs. Gundy?" Jean asked, putting her hand around the fragile bones in Harriet's hand.

Harriet held the thin cool hand as tightly as she could. "No," she said, "I'm all right now. It's you that I worry about."

"You shouldn't worry," Jean said. "Worry, sadness—what's the use of it in the end? We go," she pressed the white button, and the bed rose higher, until Harriet looked straight at Jean, "then we stop." She took her finger off the button, and the bed was still. "That's not so bad, is it?" She put her fingers around Harriet's hand again.

Harriet looked down at the chicken soup cool now in the two white bowls. She felt the apartment around her more transparent than glass now, like some soft permeable membrane with light and life moving through it as easily as air. Sitting up straight in her bed, she could see out the window, freed now from fifty-two years of venetian blinds. It was snowing. The white flakes blew up past the window into the white sky. As her eyes followed them upward, she felt so light herself that if Jean hadn't been holding her hand whatever was driving the snow upward would have drawn her up too, out over the Plaza, up into the frozen clouds. She looked into Jean's eyes.

"No," Harriet said, letting a breath go. "It doesn't seem bad at all."

TERTIARY CARE

Harry Worley first noticed her on the street—it wasn't until later he realized she lived in his building. She was standing by the public library, wearing a sort of toga made out of ripped green cloth and a matching rag tied like an Apache headband around her gray hair. But it really wasn't so much her costume that made him notice the Woman in Green as the look she gave him. Oh so imperious, like Queen Victoria, that down-a-fine-nose stare a dachshund Harry once owned had perfected to the point of intimidating Doberman pinschers. As the automatic door to the public library hissed open to receive him, she nodded, faintly, graciously, and shamed him into saying, "Have a nice day."

Not that she was the only unusual person Harry had discovered since moving to Iowa City. There was the fellow people called Smiley, whose clothes were covered with Go Hawks buttons like any good Iowa fan, but who took color Polaroids of college girls' breasts when they bent over to tie their shoes. "Smile," he'd say. And the two brothers Harry thought of as the Hitchcock Twins, because of their round stomachs and the dignified way they carried them. The Twins worked as a pair selling raffle tickets, the fatter one doing most of the talking. The other was quiet, and sometimes a bit yellow.

"It's his liver," the fatter one explained when his brother was in the Burger King getting change for Harry's ticket. "The poison backs up in his blood. That's what makes him slow."

70

"How terrible," Harry said.

"Well, it would be worse," he said, making sure his brother was still out of earshot. "The slowness keeps him from knowing how sick he is. He shouldn't know."

"It's his life," said Harry.

"But I'm the oldest. I know. I worry. It's my job."

Less self-sufficient adults and children with impairments passed through downtown too, led in long weaving lines by young women with master's degrees.

All of these people were in Iowa City for the same reason as Harry and the other old people. On the hill at the end of the walking street the University Hospital sprawled, waiting for them all. It was "Iowa's Tertiary Health Care Center." Harry wasn't sure he wanted to know what that meant. Most of the old people in Iowa City had moved off their farms—farms that had become too far down snowy unplowed roads from the safety of the hospital on the hill. They were all in outpatient care for something— bad heart, bad lungs, cancer, diabetes—otherwise they would still be at work on their land. Harry had never known a farmer to quit unless he had to.

Harry, though, was trying to get used to the hospital gradually—he volunteered for a nutrition experiment he saw advertised in the paper. He wasn't sick, and he'd never been a farmer. He'd had a State Farm Agency in Dixon for forty-two years, and he could still be in Dixon—phoning folks to ask didn't they want to add Billy to their policy since he was sixteen now, and Harry had seen him at the Dairy Keen with the Chevy. He wasn't in Dixon because his wife, Mimi, wasn't. It was her hometown. But while he was still getting plaques each year for the lowest claim rate in Iowa, Mimi had gotten suddenly old. She was seven years younger than Harry, but her bones went—so brittle she broke her back picking up a can of tomato juice at the Hy-Vee—and her lungs went—Harry bought her a La-Z-Boy so she could sleep sitting up—and then she was dead.

Even before the funeral, Dixon went back to being Mimi's town. The women who brought baked ham and scalloped potatoes by the house and then stayed to eat some talked about Mimi— how she'd worn two unmatched shoes to school one day in second grade. Without Mimi there to laugh and let Harry in on the joke, he was back to being from Seattle, a place he hadn't seen since 1936. He looked around and noticed that two of the men and three of the women had on leisure suits made out of the same blue plastic stuff, that all of them had the same strawy gray-blond hair and round red cheeks—like Mimi had, it was true, but he had loved her. Suddenly he just felt sick to death of looking at people who all looked the same.

So he sold the agency, put the house on the market too, got an atlas out of the library and sat down to figure out where he should go. Harry had liked the weather in New Caledonia, where he was stationed during the war. But though it still looked like a nice place in his *National Geographic, Time* magazine was full of pictures of the natives massacring French colonists.

Everyone in Dixon seemed to assume he wouldn't leave Iowa. Not when it had such a good Tertiary Care Facility. They kept asking him when he was moving over to Iowa City, so one day Harry said, "Next Thursday, I'm going over next Thursday." He got himself an efficiency downtown in an old stucco building, the Iowa Apartments, next to the Fire and Rescue Station. So far he couldn't say he was sorry.

Every Monday, Wednesday, and Friday morning, he got to take a list of everything he'd eaten to the second floor of the hospital, where the Nutrition Research Project shared a hall with the Core Lipid Lab. The woman in charge of Harry spent her mornings trying to find out which vitamins older people couldn't absorb, and her afternoons on which ones newborns could. Harry wasn't sure he understood how the two were connected, but he liked the idea of babies getting exactly what they needed when they sucked on their bottles. He liked the idea of bigger, better babies.

At first he went to the congregate meals at the Senior Citizens' Center, and he made up his list by copying the menus for the Center that the *Press Citizen* printed next to the school lunches. But the people there all sat and talked about somebody no-one-knew-but-them who in some town no-one-else-was-from had worn two unmatched shoes to school back in a year no-one-was-quite-sure-of. Also Harry didn't like running into other old men on the street and having them tell him to hurry down to lunch because they were having carrot cake today or not to bother because they were serving damn Italian stuff again. One day on his way back across campus from having his blood drawn at the Nutrition Project, he discovered the River Room Cafeteria. It was attached to the part of the Student Union that was a kind of Holiday Inn for all the conferences that the big medical school attracted, and so there was always a mix of people—co-eds to retired professors—seated at the tables overlooking the Iowa River. The food wasn't bad, it was cheap, and Harry liked getting to look at it firsthand before he committed himself to it.

Besides it was where the Woman in Green ate, or at least sat—at a table by the window with no food in front of her. Harry wasn't quite sure why, but he liked the idea that she watched him as he ate his meatloaf, counted out the disappointing vitamins the Project woman had given him (just the usual sort—A, B, C, D—when he'd hoped for something amazing—Q or Alpha-Zed). He liked the attention. When he got up to leave, the Woman would stand too, her eyes very blue under her green headband.

"Hello," Harry'd say, although he was leaving, and the Woman in Green would nod, graciously, before sitting back down.

After he ate lunch at the River Room, Harry usually sat for an hour or two in the walking street, bought a raffle ticket from the Hitchcock Twins, and chatted a little to whomever sat next to him on the bench. Sometime during the afternoon the Woman in Green would take up her spot by the library door. One day he was talking to the Concept Man, a black man who sold yellow mimeo-graphed sheets of his ideas, when the Woman drifted by. "That woman's crazy," the Concept Man said, shaking his head. Harry looked at the Concept Sheet he'd just bought for a nickel. The headline was *CBS, ABC, NBC, CIA Owned by Donny 666 Osmond.*

"Crazy in what way?" he asked.

The Concept Man shook his head again. "She thinks she's E.T.—you know, the Extra Terrestrial."

Harry hadn't seen the movie, but he'd read an article in *Time* magazine about how they'd done the special effects, and that gave him a pretty good idea of what the Concept Man was getting at. "You mean she thinks she was accidently left behind by her family during an outer space vacation?"

"Uh-huh, and she thinks they coming back to get her any day now." As she stood by the door to the library, the Woman in Green's blue eyes did seem focused on the horizon, on the edge of the world where Harry imagined Earth gave way to Space.

On the Tuesdays and Thursdays when he didn't have to go up to the Project to turn in his list, Harry went to lunch early. Then the Woman in Green wouldn't be inside not eating, but outside, digging. Harry would sit by the window and watch her scratching around in the bare dirt where the runoff from the eaves kept any-thing from growing. She was always kneeling, back bent, the classic stance that made Mimi say if God meant man to be a gardener he'd have given him a cast-iron hinge in the middle instead of a spine. The Woman would make a careful hole, take a piece of broken bottle or windshield, put it down so deep and no farther—half in and half out—and then pat the dirt up carefully around it. As far as Harry could tell she was planting glass.

One afternoon downtown Smiley showed Harry a Polaroid he'd taken of the Woman tending her glass garden. Smiley had gotten a closer view than Harry—maybe through a basement window—and the snapshot showed her breasts hanging loose inside her green toga. Harry was struck by how pink and young they looked.

It was after he saw her breasts, after he thought he knew all there was to know about the Woman, that he realized she lived next door to him. The Iowa Apartments were upstairs over a tanning spa, and the ones that faced the hall had screen doors, so the apartments on either side could get some cross ventilation. Most of the old people who lived in his building stayed behind their screen doors and passing down the hall was like walking past the beds of fever patients, almost invisible in their mosquito nets. Sometimes they would call out, and when Harry answered, he was in for a conversation through the screen—no one ever unlatched it and let him sit down—or a trip to the drugstore after someone's diuretics. Mrs. Patrick, who lived across the hall, was especially bad. She had an extra second or two to snare him while he unlocked his door, and she liked to send him out for laxatives, which embarrassed him.

"Mr. Worley, is that you?" she called out one day.

"Indeed," was all Harry allowed himself.

"Mr. Worley, is that *woman* in?" Harry looked up and down the hall. As far as he knew all the apartments except his and Mr. Yoder's at the end of the hall were occupied by women. He moved closer to the screen and saw Mrs. Patrick inside on her platform rocker, surrounded by the walls of what nots. His apartment had come furnished, but if Mrs. Patrick's had, the vinyl was buried by comforters.

"What lady?" he asked.

"That *woman*," Mrs. Patrick said, in a tone that made Harry remember his mother saying never-call-a-woman-a-lady-unless-you-know-she-is-one. "That woman who lives next door to you."

Harry hadn't known anyone lived behind the frosted glass door next to his. A sign on the wall next to it read: *Fire Route— Break Glass.* He thought it was a janitor's closet.

"That rag-a-bag woman," Mrs. Patrick said, her rocker squeaking. "Do you know, Mr. Worley, what she said to me?" Harry shook his head. "She said she isn't going to die. *She isn't.*" Mrs. Patrick leaned forward in her rocker, and Harry realized she was old enough to be his mother. "Why her? That's what I want to know. *Just who does she think she is?*"

Harry waited up, until the moon was shining through the screen doors into the hall, and in she came, almost waltzing up the stairs to the white door. It was the Woman in Green. She was his neighbor.

After that he waited up for her. Sometimes she came in very late, and he made himself instant coffee on his one-burner stove so he wouldn't drift off sitting in his armchair. One night he drank four or five cups, and after he heard her come in, he found he couldn't sleep. He lay awake listening to the sirens of the ambulances or fire trucks start up in the garage next door. They both had European *nee-noo-nee-noo* sirens, and Harry couldn't tell a house fire from a heart attack by the sound the way he always could in Dixon. Between disasters he listened to faint music that came from Mr. Yoder's apartment, some radio station that played big band and swing to make old people who couldn't sleep restless with memories and send young people who worked or played late off to dreamland. Then he heard her, right outside his apartment, on the fire escape. He saw the moon shine off a white ankle as it climbed past his open window. On Mr. Yoder's radio the Andrews Sisters were singing "Rum and Coca-Cola." Over his head, he heard footsteps, restless, circling. The Woman in Green was on the roof.

The day after he sat up listening to the Woman moving over his head, he was late for his Project appointment. When he pushed the up button, the hospital elevator didn't come. He pushed the button again. The double doors opened and a horrible smell came out. Something screamed. A young man backed out wheeling a cage like an aquarium with a large ape inside. Harry saw teeth, black wrinkled fists beating against the glass. He put his hands over his ears. The young man smiled as he pulled the cage out of Harry's way. In the elevator the smell was so thick Harry could taste it. Even while the woman was taking his blood, he thought he could hear the ape downstairs somewhere screaming. But when he went down the stairs on his way out, all the floors were quiet. Harry had the awful feeling the ape was dead, and it suddenly seemed as if death were a conspiracy that he had agreed to be a part of.

He was still running late when he got to the River Room for lunch. The hot lunch line was closed, and only the grill was open. Harry thought about a grilled-cheese sandwich, but he didn't feel hungry. Over the onion rings and catsup he thought he smelled ape. The Woman in Green was at her table by the window, and for once it wasn't empty. There was a plate of chicken bones in front of her, though Harry couldn't be sure she had eaten it. Harry had shied away from the fried chicken. The brown breasts with the bent wings attached seemed oddly tiny. He'd once asked the Chinese girl who was serving why they were so small. He could have sworn she said "pigeon," but the supervisor had stepped up and said, "Frozen. Pre-breaded and frozen."

Harry walked past the Woman. "Hello," he said and this time when she looked up at him, even though nothing changed in her face, he could have sworn she was smiling. She looked down, and he saw a glass hidden in her lap—a flower for her garden.

Harry didn't go to the walking street. He went back to his apartment and climbed the fire escape to the roof. It was wide and flat. Pebbles stuck in the asphalt scraped under his shoes. There was a two-foot-high parapet all around the roof and some chimneys for the furnace on the far side. In the middle was something with a sheet of tar paper draped over it. Harry lifted two bricks off the tar paper and raised a corner. Under it was a wheel, the kind of thing that might have come off the miniature windmills Iowans liked to put in their gardens, but it was mounted so that it lay flat, facing the sky not the wind. Glued to the wooden blades were pieces of glass, some clear, some red like bicycle reflectors. It looked like some artifact in *National Geographic*. Harry threw off the tar paper and stood back. The glass was bright in the sun, and tatters of cloth tied to the blades stirred in the afternoon air. One was the same green as the Woman's toga and headband, another almost as blue as her eyes. Harry gave the wheel a spin. It moved easily, almost soundlessly, and kept spinning after he thought it would stop. It was much better built than he would have guessed. He put the cover back and climbed down to his room. It felt like a different place somehow—with a prayer wheel on the roof.

When Harry got back out on the street, he thought he heard a distant siren, but all the yellow fire trucks and ambulances were in front of the station. As he went toward the walking street, the sound rose louder and higher. He thought it might be a burglar alarm, but he didn't see any police. Then he saw the slow Hitch-cock Twin. He was standing at the end of the block, outside the booth that held the instant banker machine, beating on the glass with both hands. His mouth was open, and he was screaming. There was no one in the booth, and Harry was sure it wasn't locked, but the Twin was furious, inconsolable. His screams were louder than a siren, twisted the air, but people passed by him, their eyes determinedly elsewhere. Harry broke into a trot, but the fatter Twin pushed by him, running. Harry stopped, breathing hard—the fear in the screams was contagious. Half a block away the slow Twin was flailing at his brother, driving fists into the soft expanse of his stomach. Then there was a siren, and Harry ex-pected a police car, but a yellow ambulance pulled up, hiding the Twins. Harry turned away. Right behind him was the Woman, her blue eyes open so wide they seemed like glass, one hand covering her mouth. She blinked, looked at him. "I'm afraid of death," she said, her voice soft behind her fingers. And Harry realized he was too.

That night the moon was full—it was bright enough in his apartment to read a newspaper. Harry remembered reading in a *World Book* encyclopedia that, when the moon was full, Romans didn't go to bed at all but went walking around in the city visiting friends, and the shopkeepers would throw open the stalls just like it was day—a holiday. It certainly didn't seem possible to sleep when the light was everywhere, was so peculiarly shadowless. Harry lay on his bed waiting for the Woman to come in, trusting the moonlight this time instead of coffee. Down the hall Mr. Yoder's radio played songs with "moon" in them, "Shine on Harvest Moon," "Moon River," and finally Bing singing "Moonlight Becomes You"—

> You're all dressed up to go dreaming—
> Now don't tell me I'm wrong.
> What a night to go dreaming—
> Mind if I come along?

It was too much of a lullaby for Harry, and he closed his eyes to the moonlight.

He woke when he heard her on the fire escape. It was late. The moon was high in the sky, and his room was only faintly lit. He heard her overhead and imagined the wheel uncovered, scattering the light of the moon and the stars. He was up the fire escape before he really had time to think, as if he were sleepwalking, and there she was. The wheel *was* turning, and she was turning too, around and around, dancing on the roof over Mrs. Patrick's head, Mr. Yoder's radio, Harry's empty bed. But she wasn't dancing like some Hindu goddess, all scarves and bare feet. She was just dancing like Mimi danced, dancing as if she had been in the dancing class with him back at Mrs. Porter's School in Seattle.

One—two—three, One—two—three. Around she spun with her eyes closed, her arms held out but empty—as if too few boys had shown up for the class. The wheel turned soundlessly, but Harry still seemed to hear music—

> Moonlight becomes you—
> It goes with your hair.

She swept past Harry, and suddenly he was dancing, her green headband almost resting on his shoulder.

> You certainly know
> The right thing to wear.

She looked at him with eyes like blue moons. "It isn't fair that that we have to die, is it?" she asked.

"No," Harry said, dipping her, leading her, "it isn't." Down below, on earth, a siren started.

LA MORT AU MOYEN ÂGE

I wake up. This surprises me. I don't remember going to bed.
Wait. I am not in bed. I am sitting, slumped face down,
at my dining room table. I open my left eye and see a small puddle
left by the steam of my breath on the cherry veneer.

Enough of this. I try to sit up. It doesn't seem possible. Asleep.
I wait for the pins and needles to start. Instead my left hand comes
to my rescue, and pushing, palm flat on the table, it lifts my useless right side and numb face until I am sitting upright in the
chair. There.

I wiggle the fingers on my left hand. They wiggle willingly and
with great vigor. Good. I tap my left foot. *Tap-tap-heel-toe-tap.*
Even better.

I look down at my right hand still asleep on the table. There is
a piece of paper crumbled in its fist.

Open.

It is recalcitrant. *I don't wanna. I don't wanna.*

Gimme, gimme, gimme, I order. It twitches, an obvious play
for sympathy. I speak with my left hand. *Kill,* I say.

My left hand goes to it with the enthusiasm of a long-neglected
younger brother. It pries open my right fist, finger by finger, and
returns bearing the paper in triumph. My right hand just lies
there, palm up, fingers slightly curled—a joke. What's a W? A
dead M.

The piece of paper is not blank, but to my right eye it seems to be written in an infinitely foreign language. Urdu? Farsi? Perhaps it is a letter for Dr. Singh, whose mailbox is below mine.

I hold the letter nearer to my left eye. That's better. Obviously English, although a pretty smeary job of typing. The letters bob and blur when I blink. A basic case of instability here. Yes.

Dear Esther Herbert,

Well, then it is my letter.

We regret to inform you that we are unable to use . . .

CRACK. POCK. Something pops inside my skull behind my right eye. POCK-CRACK, like a carapace of a tromped-on cockroach. The letter really is too damn dim to read. I feel sick. No, better now.

How odd. I think my brain cells are exploding. Maybe I'd better stop thinking. 100, 99, 98, 97, 96, 95. Calm.

I remember what is in the letter. I remember reading it sitting at the dining room table. It is a rejection letter from the University Press. They find there is no current need for a critical edition of Edward Topsell's *Historie of the Foure-Footed Beastes* with an attached examination of its relation to the German bestiary of Conrad Gesner. They hint that they find my credentials thin— that if I enlisted the aid of an older and more established scholar in my field—well then . . . They suggest the head of my department, Dr. Klaus Heidleman, Jr.

I used to date Klaus Heidleman, Sr.—and he was a year behind me in school.

POCK-CRACK-POCK. I have had, am having, a stroke. A cerebral accident. Crash. My exploding cockroach dying brain cells can no longer conceal this information from me. Stroke.

POCK. I am having a stroke. CRACK. My work of twenty-five years has been summarily dismissed. Physical deterioration. Intellectual rejection. I have been trashed.

Ah, to dismiss your great *Historie*, Edward. A work

Describing the true and lively figure of every Beaste, with a discourse of their several Names, Conditions, Kindes, Vertues (both naturall and medicinall) Countries of their breed, their love and hate of Mankinde and the wonderful worke of God on their Creation, Preservation, and Destruction.

Crack. I can't remember, quite remember what started me with you, Edward of the *Foure-Footed Beastes*. What was behind that first impulse?

Maude, it was Maude. Maude who has been departmental secretary for thirty-six years. Maude who wanted me to publish and become a full professor. Maude, who loves me, whose project is killing me. Mort. Mort. Maude. Maude.

We thought we would be middle-aged forever, Maude. Prime stuff. Around and around in the old Moyen Age. Pock and Crack, Maude, I'm old. I want to retire with you and raise Turkish Van cats and bird-sized poodles.

I must get to the car. I must get to the College. I must get to Maude.

I stand up. It is not as difficult as I had imagined. My right leg is less disobedient than my right hand. The leg works. It steps, sweeps, the knee locked tight. My left leg is impatient. It dance steps, two times for every slow right stride.

Come on, come on, come on, it taps nervously.

I reach the door. Luckily I live in a house that was just waiting for me to grow old. There are no steps. The sidewalk stretches smooth and level all the way to the drive. To the car. To the car that is the car of my husband. Both of my eyes together agree that the car of my husband is an unsightly hunk of junk. Rust on what's there—trunk, hood. Rust the thief of what's not there—fenders, floorboards. Doors that won't stay open and won't stay shut. This is the car of my husband. It is his fault; I feel that clearly as I look at the shameful thing. Yet it is an old car—how long since I have had a husband?—still it is his fault, his failed responsibility—what was the name of my husband?

It is not easy to get the key in the ignition with my left hand. My left hand is an Unskilled Trainee. The car starts. The car of my husband rolls, runs, motivates, and my left hand, with slight aid from my veteran right knee, instructs the car—*To the College.*

Luckily I live on a street that was just waiting for me to get old. It is very straight, well-paved. The speed limit is thirty-five.

I rest my right hand, still uselessly, fetally curved, on the bungee cord that I use to keep the passenger door closed. It stretches from the door's useless handle to the useless hole where the car of my husband does not have a radio. The bungee cord is green with a threading of purple. My hand is white with a threading of purple.

My slow but steady right foot has control of the accelerator pedal, but I let my left foot handle the brakes. My left foot taps, impatient for stop signs and sudden children on tricycles.

We continue to move.

I find it easier to stay between the yellow lines if I close my right eye. *Wink-blink.* To my right eye something dark and impenetrably hard seems to be looming just beyond the edge of its poor sluggish sight. I find this distracting. My left eye is appointed watch of the day.

It is actually a very nice day. Sun, blue sky, so on. Relax.

My left eye sees someone standing in the road. In my surprise I allow my right eye to open. It is terrified. My overeager left foot hits the brakes hard. My right foot stays on the gas. All four bald tires scream. *MERCY!*

I have accidentally stopped the car in front of a hitchhiker. The hitchhiker smiles and tugs at my passenger door. His attempts at the door make the green and purple bungee cord stretch and contract. The door stays shut but my right hand bobs up and down in an involuntary helpless wave.

"Hi," says the hitchhiker, getting a little concerned about the elasticity of the door. He has long hair, a beard, a red bandanna. He is a visual anachronism. He is the kind of student who, for one brief period in the late sixties, overloaded my classes because they liked to hear what they didn't understand.

My left hand, in a rush of nostalgia, unhooks the bungee and lets the anachronism in.

"Hi," he says again.

My left hand rehooks the bungee. This pins the hitchhiker to the seat—Passive Restraint System—and makes him nervous.

"Hi," he says to the bungee.

Perhaps he is not a native speaker of English.

"Are you a student?" I ask. My lips stick together. My tongue drags. I sound Portuguese.

The hitchhiker's head waggles in a sort of circular maybe. His head continues to waggle as he points at the front windshield. My left hand is driving us down the rough grassy shoulder. My right knee nudges us back onto the pavement. The hitchhiker's head stops bobbing.

It is difficult to watch him and the road with my left eye. I take a peek with my right eye. This is a mistake. He is huge and hairy. I see the shadow of vicious teeth under his beard. Perhaps he is not human. I remember a test for this very thing from Topsell's chapter, "Of the Ape":

> And as the body of the Ape is ridiculous by reason of its indecent likeness and imitation of Man, so is his soule or spirit. A certain Ape after a shipwreck swimming to lande, was seene by a Countrey man, and thinking him to be a man in the water, gave him a hand to save him, yet in the meane time asked him what Countrey man he was, who answered that he was an Athenian: Well saide the man, Doost thou know Pireus (which is a port of

Athens) very well saide the Ape, and his wife, friends, and children, whereat the man being moved did what he could to drown him.

"Doost thou know Pireus?" I ask with a painful effort at clarity of pronunciation.

The hitchhiker waggles his head. "Sure," he says, "I took a class from him."

My left hand flashes out to unhook the bungee. The car bumps off the pavement and tilts crazily to the right. The door bangs open. The hitchhiker tumbles out, the bungee cord lashing at him as he goes.

"HA!" I say to the flapping door, "Pireus, indeed."

My left hand is too busy getting us back on the road to catch the flailing bungee, and the door bangs wildly as my right foot gases us toward the College.

The hitchhiker menace is gone. It really is a nice day. Birds, flowers, clouds, etc. Maude is partial to Epithalamia. I sing to Maude.

"Oh Maude of the red lipstick and blue hair—oh many colored Maude—Oh Maude of the sixty words per minute with one mistake—Oh Maude, Esther is coming . . ."

I sing this to the tune of "Strangers in the Night," which is Maude's favorite song.

My right foot presses the accelerator pedal with desire for Maude.

Not far now, I encourage my foot.

I hear a roar from behind, and then a *whoosh-vroom* of wind slides the car sideways onto the shoulder. A black Cadillac vaults by. It honks. Something inside waves.

My left hand exercises its increased skill and pulls the car back up on the road.

The black car is the car of Dr. Klaus Heidleman, Jr., the chairman of the department and vice president of the Alumni Boosters Association. I remember he is returning from a Boosters convention in Las Vegas.

I smell his rich exhaust.

"You're a Gulon, Heidleman!" I shout at his rear bumper.

My left hand is very angry. My left foot eases over and adds its weight to the gas pedal. I scream passages from the Historie at the black car of Dr. Heidleman.

A Gulon is a devouring and unprofitable creature, having sharper teeth than other creatures, and it feedeth upon dead carkases.

When it hath found a dead carkas he eateth thereof so violently, that his belly standeth out like a bell; then he seeketh some narrow passage betwixt two trees, and there draweth through his body, by pressing thereof, he driveth out the meate which he hath eaten; and being so emptied returneth and devoreth as much as he did before, and goeth again and emptyeth himself in the former manner; and so continueth eating and emptying until al is eaten. It may be that God has ordained such a creature in certaine countries, to express the abominable gluttony of the men of that countrie.

My speed is reckless. I praise the car of my husband, and spurred on by this unheard of grace, its cylinders flog us into the fray. We draw closer to the black car that is the car of Dr. Heidleman. Again I smell its heavy exhaust. My left hand pulls us out to pass. Dr. Heidleman's shiny face glares at us through sun-tinted windows.

BASH. My left hand swings us over against the black Caddy. I open my right eye, and my right eye says, *Yes. This is the awful black thing that we feared.*

BAM. BASH. The car of my husband throws itself against the car of Dr. Heidleman in a fit of class consciousness. His car swerves, lurches off the road, crushing the barrier fence. It tries to squeeze itself through a Volkswagen-size gap between two Ponderosa pines. CRUNCH. GROAN. It is too fat. It squeals. The trunk bangs open and ejects fat luggage. Playful pine cones bounce off the wrinkled roof of the car of Dr. Heidleman. I wave.

The car carries me to my faculty parking space with one last valve-wrenching effort. SPOCK-CRACK, it goes as I leave it in a crowd of people who are discussing calling the fire department.

I enter the Department Office. Maude, her purple pants-suited back to me, is carefully painting peaks on her lip with a red, red lipstick. She examines her handiwork in a small round magnifying mirror. She sees my reflection in the mirror, sees in its 2× surface the limp, the dropping eye and lip, the trail of saliva that quivers as I say, "Maude, Maude."

Maude's hand jerks and the red lipstick cuts across her cheek. A gashing smile.

The hand that wrecked the car that was the car of Dr. Heidleman hangs limp and humble at my side. I stare at my reflection in the mirror. What think you, Edward?

It is said that the Unicorn above all other creatures soe reverences Virgins and young Maides, and that many times at the sight of them they grow tame, and come and sleep beside them.

"Oh, Maude, Maude," I say, "the true Unicorn hath ever been in doubt."

Maude raises her arms to me, and I slump into her lap.

"*La Mort au Moyen Âge*," I say to Maude's lap. She bends over me, her breasts tricot pillows for the back of my head.

THE HISTORY OF THE CHURCH IN AMEREICA

The post office slid out of town last night. I heard it go, and when I went out this morning, I saw it had taken a chunk of Prophet Street with it down the mountain. I stood at the edge of the slide, looking down. The Zion City Post Office was just so much kindling in the valley below, mingling with the older debris from the *Light of the World* office, the Daily Bread Bakery, and the Holy Harmony Hotel. Letters flew like birds across the valley on the morning wind. Letters set free after seventy years waiting in P.O. boxes for people who left in the Desertion and were never coming back. I watched as a letter flew too close to the open flame of a gas well and burned, bright as a wish.

I felt the messenger come up beside me as I stood looking down. I knew who he was, of course. He was dressed all in white, just like me, though the red dust of Zion had stained the hem of my dress beyond bleaching, and he looked fresh off a tennis court. He also looked like a boy to me—but then I'm eighty-five and can't judge anymore. He'd come in a Jeep that was parked by the Divine Will General Store, on the other side of what was left of Prophet Street. The Jeep was green and tan, so I guessed he rented it. A Church car would be as white as us.

"The whole town," I said to him, "is moving down the mountain at a rate of two inches a year." A man from the geodetic survey had told me this.

"Salem, Sister Ruth," he said. "I have a message for you." He didn't want to be sidetracked.

"I know," I said. "Come on over to the house."

The Church hadn't sent a messenger in years. They used to come all the time after the Desertion left my mother, my brother Nils, and me alone in Zion City. It was embarrassing for them to have their new city in Oregon but not their Prophet's body or family or papers, which were all still drying up in the desert. Mother always sent the messengers away. When she died, they stopped coming. But here was this boy.

Temple House, where I live, was my father's house. It's four doors up Prophet Street from where the post office took the plunge. That's why the street is called that—because my father was a prophet, and his house was on it. Also, he named it.

The messenger followed me calmly enough past the Mac-Alisters' (sure to follow the post office), the Johansons' (floor missing), the Mullers' (holding on), but he stopped at the threshold of Temple House. There was no door, of course, but he should be used to that. Or maybe it's true what I hear about their using sliding-glass doors in Oregon to get around this tenet. But then it does rain an awful lot out there. Here all that comes through the open doorway is dust.

"Come on in," I said, and he did. He sat down on the washing bench and took off his shoes while I poured some water in the basin. "Blood of the Lamb," I said, washing first his right foot then his left. They were as soft as puppies. I started to dry them, but he turned ticklish, so I gave him the guest towel.

"I think you'd be used to it," I said.

"At home," he said, putting on his shoes, "we do ritual sprinkling."

"Do tell," I said. I went across to my rocker, but the boy stayed near the door. It made him nervous to hear my footsteps, hollow on a floor hung like a drum over the valley. "I checked the supports this morning," I told him, though I did no such thing. It wouldn't have done any good. I'd checked the post office not two days before. The messenger crossed the room on his puppy feet, walking oh so soft, and handed me what he'd brought all this way. There was one big white letter with a silly wax seal and then a regular one with a postage stamp—though it had been a while since a letter got to Zion that way. I set them on the reading table.

"I'm to wait for a reply," he said, edging back toward the doorway and solid ground.

"I need to read them," I said. "I need a day." He stopped, looking handsome and unhappy and young. "Why don't you go down to Sedona and come back tomorrow? I can't let you sleep here on the Sabbath anyway—you being a heretic and all." Oh, he looked so startled to be called that. The old divisions weren't real to him.

But he was relieved too. "Tomorrow, Sister Ruth," he said, actually bowing as he left.

"If I was you," I called after him, "I'd watch that road down the mountain."

It was on March 25, 1885, my father received the first Visitation. He was a law clerk in the District of Columbia, and he was busy copying some precedents about hearsay testimony. It was snowing hard, late in the year for D.C., and he had pretty much decided to work all night rather than try a cold, blinding walk home. About two o'clock, there was a knock at the door. When my father said, "Come in," he looked up to see himself coming through the door—followed by himself, and himself, and himself, and himself. My father put down his pen. The office began to fill up.

Then Jesus came in. Father recognized him right away, even in a white summer suit. Jesus was taller and more handsome than the men he squeezed past to Father's desk, in exactly the same proportion that he was taller and more handsome than Father. Jesus held his hands out to him.

"If you would save yourself," he said, "you could save this many people." He spread his arms wide, and Father saw that everyone in the room had on a white suit and that there were a lot of them, more than he could count, more than should have fit in his office. Their new suits were blinding. In them they didn't look quite so homely or short next to Jesus. They were smiling, almost handsome.

It wasn't until Father got home that he realized his suit, which had been a gray pinstripe, was white now too. In fact every suit in his closet was white, and every hat, even each sock in every pair of socks. He got out his Bible and went through it marking every mention of white. I learned what he found in Sabbath School:

Q: Whose countenance is like lightning,
    whose raiment white as snow?
A: Jesus, Jesus, Lamb of God.

Q: Who have washed their robes, and made
    them white in the blood of the Lamb?
A: We have, Jesus, we have.

Father was wearing one of the white suits when he met Mother, though it was summer then, so she didn't notice his white clothes as much as his white hair, something he'd gained from the Second Visitation in April. He'd been about asleep when he heard a noise at his door. Not a knock, just a sort of rustle. He was tired and didn't want to get up, but the noise was so soft and so odd, he finally got curious. He stood on a chair and looked over the transom. In the hall, nuzzling his door, was a lamb. A pretty much newborn lamb, although as a city man he wasn't too sure a judge.

He opened his door to the lamb, and it knelt down before him. Father sat on the chair. The lamb began to lick Father's feet. Toe to heel, its tongue as warm as any heart.

Which is why we wash our Brethren's feet. Wash and not sprinkle.

Father explained all this to Mother over several walks on the Mall. Mother was a file girl at the Library of Congress. One day by the Potomac, Father said, "Look at those fine houses with their shades drawn down and their doors locked tight. Would they hear the Last Trump, let alone a Lamb at the door? What could they have to hide but sin? Evil may go on in an apartment in the city, but at least it stands a chance of being found out by those who could intervene in Christ's name. When I see a mansion, alone on a great lawn, or a farmhouse, an island in a sea of corn, then I think—there the light of God is kept under a bushel."

To his surprise, Mother began to cry. She threw herself down on the grass and wept until she made herself sick. Father pressed his fingers to her temples. "In the end," he said to her, "God will wipe away all the tears from our eyes."

When she could sit up, she told him about a night she remembered from when she was small. Her father had been beating her mother and maybe her brother Nils too. Her mother ran with them through the fields to the neighbors. It was snowing, a long way. When they got there, the neighbors were gone, but the door wasn't locked. They sat on the floor in the hall, waiting. Or had they hidden in the barn? Once they hid in a church. Because this had happened before. Always the neighbor or someone found them. The neighbor talked to her mother. His voice low, a river of gravel. Her mother's like panting. Then he loaded them on his wagon, and they rode over frozen roads to the farmhouse. She felt the strength in his hands as he lifted her from the wagon. Then he drove his team away, never looking back. They were left standing in the snow outside their house.

"Baby," her mother said, breathing the word in her ear, "go in the house and ask your father if he loves me."

She went. "Do you love Ma?" she asked him.

"I love her," her father said, "but that won't save her."

When she went back out, her mother was on her knees, whispering in Nils's ear. Then her mother went into the house. They waited outside for a long time. Longer, it seemed to her, than it took to get to the neighbors'.

Leaning on the locked barn door, she fell asleep. Nils pulled on her hand. "Come on," he said, making her run. "Come on, stupid!" They crossed the field again, came to the railroad tracks. A train came, slow, slow. She would guess, looking back, that the grade was steep and the tracks icy. Nils lifted her up, his hands tiny compared to the neighbor's, to her father's. Lifted her up into an open box car and let go.

When she looked back, Nils was a faint smudge in the snow.

That very night Father received the Vision of Zion. He was dressed to take Mother to a concert at the bandshell but when he went outside, he found himself in a city high on a mountain. It was night there too, but not dark. Light shone out of all the windows and doorways, not blocked by curtains or doors. In and out of the open doorways wandered sheep—chatting, laughing, calling *Salem* to each other as both hello and good-bye.

"Salem," one of them said, and then Father noticed he was a sheep too. His wool curled tight around his face and feet and was warmer and more comfortable than any nightgown he'd ever owned.

"Salem," said another sheep who Father recognized at once as Jesus because his wool was whiter than snow, as white as light. "You are the light of the world," Jesus said. "Will you build me a city that is set on a hill and cannot be hid?"

"You bet," said Father.

I think Father picked Arizona for Zion City because he'd seen pictures of Hopi villages perched on mesas. Not that Father led the Church that far west to start with. He founded the Church on January 1, 1886, and married Mother the next day. After that, every year found them camped further west—New Zion, West Virginia—Zionburg, Indiana—Zionville, Missouri. My brother Eli was born in Missouri. I wasn't born until the Last Camp of the Exodus but I know its trials the same way I know Mother was in labor with me for a week or that I was born with one tooth. There were Forty Martyrs to the Exodus—one for every day Christ spent in the Wilderness. The night I was born the last martyr, Baby Adam, got carried off by coyotes.

In the desert Jesus appeared to Father and delivered him a prophecy, jotting it down on a hundred-dollar bill so he wouldn't lose it. Carrying that bill, Father said, was a daily choice between God and Mammon. On June 3, 1899, Father consecrated Zion City and revealed the prophecy, writing it in the sand:

IN ZION WILL BE BORN A NEW MAN
SON OF THE LAMB OF GOD.

All the Brethren were gathered on the top of the mountain, except Mother who was in labor with my brother Nils. There was a slight pause, while people read, then a round of applause.

"I guess," Brother Hills said to Father, "that we're all New Men and Sons of the Lamb of God. And proud of it."

"I wouldn't be too sure," Father said. "If it had already happened it wouldn't be a prophecy." He had the cemetery laid out on that spot, at the very top of Zion. So each time the Brethren looked up, they would be reminded of the limit of man's understanding.

But a lot was happening. By January when the new century came in, the Brethren had nailed a city onto Zion's red slope. That summer the water pipe up from the valley was finished, and by the fall of 1900, Zion was the third largest city in Arizona. By the time I was old enough to notice, I lived in a grand place. The houses climbed up the mountain, all painted the whitest of whites, all covered with green vines that gave shade in the absence of trees. Mother always said Zion looked like Italy, though she'd never been there. I can understand that—when I imagine Italy, it looks like Zion.

More souls joined the Church every day. To live in openness, no doors, no curtains. "For nothing is secret, that shall not be made manifest; neither any thing hid, that shall not be known." On Sabbath Eve, we lit candles in every window, and Zion City outshone the desert stars.

Then on October 13, 1907, someone threw a stick of lit dynamite under the wagon Father was driving up the mountain. He wasn't blown straight to Heaven or to atoms—two tales I hear they tell in Oregon to explain where his body is. But he was blown high in the air. The wagon and the horse, Bill, whom I was fond of, went over and over down the mountain. It was the first time I knew a horse could scream. When the Brethren came running, they found Father dead. His right arm pointing up at Heaven.

I remember both of Father's funerals. For the Church funeral the whole of Zion rose before dawn and marched with candles up toward the growing light and the cemetery. But the coffin was empty. Father believed in bodily resurrection, and Mother was afraid the grave might be desecrated, his body carried off who knows where, and then on Resurrection Morn, there she'd be—reborn but alone. We folded the hundred-dollar bill with the prophecy in his upraised hand, wrapped him in white linen, and carried him at midnight to where my oldest brother Eli had prepared the grave. Mother made Eli and Nils hold Father up, and she took off his shoes and washed his feet one last time.

"Salem, Husband," she said. "Salem."

After the Martyrdom, all Hell broke loose in the Church. The talk was that Father had been murdered over mineral rights. There wasn't much farming to do in Zion City. Poor mountain soil is one of the reasons most people live in valleys. Father had been considering opening a mine. Maybe, people said, the copper companies hadn't liked that.

A lot of folks, led by the Church Treasurer, Brother Hill, wanted to leave Zion City. Maybe moving had gotten to be a habit. Maybe, like the rest of America, the Brethren were itching to get as far west as it was possible to go. Mother said no. Brother Hill said the Brethren should elect a Shepherd to lead them. Then during Sabbath Meeting, my youngest brother, Nils, stood up and told the whole Church how Father had called him into the *Light of the World* office the afternoon before he was martyred and laid his hands on Nils's head and cried out to God that this was the One of Whom the Prophecy had spoken, Who would lead the Church to the End of Time and live to see the Resurrection of the Dead. "This one, Lord," he said, "has got the brains for it."

Nils was seven then, and he caused quite a stir. I don't know what to think of him, even now, looking back. Mother named him Nils, and Father hadn't the heart to ask her to change it. His unbiblical name set him apart from Eli and me—made him seem like he was an orphan from some other family. Maybe he thought that too. He was round-faced and silent. Until the day he stood up in meeting, I don't think anyone but Mother had had two thoughts about him to rub together.

Eli was twenty-one then. He and Father had worked together almost every day. It was odd luck he hadn't been martyred too, and he took it hard. Eli was like that. He'd been born without saliva glands in his mouth. When he ate, he had to dip each piece of his food in a bowl of water, like a raccoon. And he couldn't say more than a dozen words without a drink of water. It made him shy.

Eli sat on that Sabbath and listened to Nils's story. Then he stood and said the only words I ever heard him say in Meeting besides *amen*. "Bunk," he said, "pure bunk." He walked out, and, by the time we got home, he'd packed his things and moved into the Divine Will General Store.

Nils's pronouncement split the Church. Or, at least, it failed to hold the Church together. Some said, "Maybe he is the next Prophet, but he won't be shaving for another ten years." Others, "How do we know the boy didn't just say what his Ma told him to say?" Brother Hill sent some scouts out to Oregon, and, when they came back, the only word you could hear in town was green. Oregon was green. Green trees. Green grass. It was like people turned into crickets, all making the same sound. Not one tongue praising the *white, white Lamb*.

The Desertion took place January 1, 1908, the Twenty-Eighth Anniversary of the Founding of the Church. The night before, Eli had come to the back door to see me.

"Come with me, Ruthie," he said. "I'm lonely without you."

"You know I can't," I said. I wasn't the kind of child who even played at running away. I couldn't imagine leaving my mother, or Zion.

"Salem then, Ruthie," he said.

I gave him a dipper of water, but he had nothing more to say. "Salem, Eli," I said, and he was gone.

The Desertion made such a racket, wheels and hooves and shoes rattling down the rock road to the valley. After that when someone left Zion, it was just an echo of that great noise. Mother made Nils and me sit at the table with breakfast in front of us. When she thought I was looking out the window, she started a long prayer and made us kneel. But after they were gone and she let us stand, I ran up Cherubim, Seraphim, and Perpetual Crier streets to the cemetery. I waved and waved to Eli, though we had already said good-bye, though I knew he couldn't see me. A red dust hung over the valley. There were beautiful sunsets for days.

Only two other families stayed with us—the Johansons and the Mullers. They moved into the houses next to Temple House. Then it was quiet, for quite a long while. Brother Johanson kept the empty houses painted white, but with no one to pour bath water on their roots, the vines withered. They rattled in the wind until they dried to dust and blew away. We couldn't keep Sabbath lights in all the windows for fear of fire, but we lit up Prophet Street as best we could, each of us tending two houses. Nils went back to being quiet. He didn't speak in Meeting. He sat mostly, here or there around town. Once I found him on a sack of mail in the post office. I asked him what he was doing.

"Doing?" he said. "I'm not *doing* anything."

He was waiting for his call, Mother decided. Father had been called. When Nils was ready, he too would rise to lead the Church.

Three years after the Desertion, the first messenger came back to Zion City from Oregon—from new Zionopolis. Mother had Brother Muller send him away, his feet unwashed. Every year after that, one came and was sent away, the message they brought so persistently undelivered. But Mother swore she'd seen a light in the cemetery—they were after her husband's body. One Sabbath, Brother Johanson fell through the *Light of the World* floor, and, after his leg healed, the Johansons left. Wheels and hooves and feet going down the mountain again. I grew up. Nils grew up. Zion City inched closer to the valley.

Then in the summer of 1914, when I was nineteen, Mother rented half of Zion City to a collective of Utopians—French Utopians. She was afraid the houses would fall down before Nils had a chance to fill them with new Brethren. The Utopians moved in with the help of motor cars, the first we'd seen, and changed the name of Cherubim Street to Avenue de la Félicité and Seraphim Street to Rue de l'Humanité. Their leader was the scientist and poet Claude Achille Lautréamont, and he brought with him his wife, his secretary, his maid, his cook, his daughter, and fourteen fellow Utopians.

The first I met was Odile, the cook, who at fifty looked old to me then. At the time, I was troubled by the idea of dreams. The Church taught us to lead transparent lives, our thoughts open to God and each other. But my dreams kept their secrets even from me. I was passing up Rue de l'Humanité on the way to the cemetery when Odile called out to me, "Don't dream of butter. It means unwholesome love."

Twenty-five years later, after Odile dreamed of holding a baby, she wrote this list for me:

> Q: I Dreamed of a Baby
> A: Death in Your Sleep
>
> Q: I Dreamed of Meat
> A: Fortunate if Cooked for Others
>
> Q: I Dreamed of Poison
> A: Loss from Dishonesty
>
> Q: I Dreamed of a Bicycle
> A: You will Realize All Your Desires
>
> Q: I Dreamed I was Mad
> A: A Good Sign for All

But that day, I said to the woman in black who had called out to me, "I didn't dream of butter. I dreamed of an airplane."

She shook her head. "Airplanes are angels," she said. "To dream of an angel . . ."

But the daughter, Madeleine, came out in a dress as red as the blood in my heart. "Merde!" she said. "All dreams are sexual. If what you dream about is longer than it is wide, then it's a penis. If it's round, it's a breast."

"What about wombs?" Odile said. Madeleine shrugged.

"Who dreams of that?"

"Well, don't dream of oranges then," Odile said. "An orange means a baby on the way."

The airplane in my dream had dropped oranges like bombs— but I was more interested in hearing what Madeleine might say. Up until she said so, I hadn't known a penis was longer than it was wide. We went in her father's house, and she let me try on her dress. The fabric was stiff compared to my white cotton, but oh the feel of it. It made me aware for the first time that I had skin all over my body. Madeleine got out a mirror and held it for me to look at myself. But all I could see was the dress, redder than blood. I looked like a ghost, a corpse. It scared me to death.

"It's not your color," Madeleine said, "that's all."

I remember things like that, from my days with Madeleine. We played games. Silly ones mostly, too young for our age. But I'd never had a playmate, and maybe Madeleine hadn't either. One afternoon we went swimming in the spring at the foot of the mountain. We were mermaids, Pearl and Coral, and swam with our legs crossed like flippers.

"Oh Pearl, dear," Madeleine as mermaid called to me.

"Yes, Coral, honey?" I called back, swimming closer.

"Did you know that those land women have penises just like their men?" she said.

"What?" I said.

"You're cheating, Ruthie." I was standing now, legs uncrossed.

"I don't care," I said. "I want to know what you're talking about."

In the end she convinced me to look for myself. How strange that I had washed myself every day and never noticed it. Now there it was, peeking out at me like the shyest of tadpoles. Hello, out there, hello.

"It's your *petite pine*." Madeleine said. And so it was.

Whenever he could, Madeleine's father quizzed me about the Church. He insisted I call him Claude as the other Utopians did, though Madeleine wasn't allowed to. He took elaborate notes that looked to me more like doodles. That, he explained, when I asked about a particularly squiggly corkscrew, was because he was thinking in cycles, not lines. History was not a line. The history of the Church, for example, was a wheel within a wheel. All over America, religions sprang up and rolled west. Indians were one of the Lost Tribes of Israel. Jesus Christ had secretly returned. Israel in The Book of Revelation was really America. A Second Reformation. New religions for a new continent. Always rolling west. Faith brought men into land that Reason would have said *non, merci* to.

Even though Claude used words like Anglo-Israelianism, as he spoke I saw the Church and the Mormons and the Jehovah's Witnesses as if they were mountains, strata, rising and falling in a great upheaval, shaping a continent. "It's all part of God's plan?" I asked.

"It's all Love!" Claude said. "Love comes from men's hearts and moves mountains!"

"Oh, Claude!" Madeleine clutched her breast and rolled her eyes.

Her father slapped her. Madeleine's face turned as red as her dress. She stood up. "Well, all I care about is when love is going to grow wings and fly me out of here!" she said, turned on one heel and left.

Madeleine was more interested in telling me about the world than hearing more about the Church. But no matter how much she described Paris or Rome, Vienna, Prague, I saw them as bigger versions of Zion City. Paris climbed a mountain from the Louvre to the Moulin Rouge. I put the Seine at the bottom, where our spring was.

"No, no," Madeleine said. "Like this." She made a map of Paris on the kitchen table with trails of salt. "Flat," she said. "The Champs Élysées—flat. The Rive Gauche is flat. Only Montmartre," she poured out a mound of sugar, "and Montparnasse climb hills."

That night, I dreamed I visited Paris. The buildings were so flat, they were lines on the ground. "And the people were as flat as hats," I told Odile.

"To dream of hats," she said, "means heartbreak."

That was the morning of Bastille Day, July 14, 1919. The day Madeleine disappeared. The day Nils disappeared. Claude was furious. He suggested to Mother what he thought Nils was doing to his Madeleine. Mother threw the rent money in his face and said she was sorry it was only paper. Nils, Mother announced, had gone into the Wilderness to ready himself. He would be gone forty days. The Utopians had that long to pack.

Claude left the next day, taking his secretary. He told Odile he was going to hire a Pinkerton man. After a week, he sent for Madame Lautréamont, and she left with the maid. The Utopians exchanged addresses and went on to other experiments. Odile stayed. She put away her black dresses and sewed up new white ones. She had dreamed, she said, of my father. He danced with her on a cloud. "To dance in a dream," she said, "means happiness in service."

I couldn't believe Madeleine had left without telling me. I hung around the post office waiting for the mail, though it came only once a week. I didn't believe she and Nils had gone off together. When had Madeleine been out of my sight long enough to talk to him? Still, for the second time, Nils had gone and spoiled everything. Like he was born to it.

On August 13, Nils's forty days in the Wilderness were up. Mother took a pair of opera glasses the Utopians had left and climbed to the cemetery to keep watch. From there she must have seen the Mullers leave. But when she came down, long after dark, she went to bed without a word. She stayed there. Often as not, I slept on the empty mail sacks in the post office. Odile fed us both. On mail days, I would go through all the letters looking for word from Madeleine. After I left, Mother would come to check for one from Nils. When there was nothing—and there was always nothing—I didn't bother to stuff the letters into boxes already full of abandoned letters. The post office had a back door, the only door in town. The building had been built backward by mistake, and the Brethren were afraid a child might fall out the doorway and off the mountain. I would open the back door, and sitting with my feet cooling in space, sail the useless mail out on the warm updraft from the valley.

One day Mother found a newspaper in the mail bag addressed to her. It was the *Zionopolis Light of the World*. She started to put it down, but then she saw Nils's name. He'd written a letter to the editor.

He didn't believe God had talked to his father. He didn't even believe his father was his father. "My mother sleeps with Satan and suckles him with an extra tit. My mother murdered her own husband so I could be Prophet. I wish," Nils wrote, "I had killed her."

Mother rolled up the newspaper and put it back in the mail bag. Then she opened the back door and stepped out. A prospector below thought she was a falling angel—shot down by a blast from Hell. Joe was the only convert Mother ever made.

He brought Mother's body up on his donkey, Cumi.

"Salem," Odile said. She washed one of his feet, and I washed the other. After the funeral, he told us a story as the candles burned down. One night, a long while ago, he'd been south with a partner. The moon came up with a ring around it like a lasso. It shone so bright, cactus started blooming. Then they heard music. So high up, it made your ears itch. Made Cumi crazy. She took off, and they followed her. They found her leaning against a giant saguaro, watching a woman nurse a baby. Sitting balanced on the arms of the cactus were two men wearing robes whiter than any Chinaman could make them. Each also wore three pairs of wings—one pair to cover his feet, one to cover his eyes, and another to fly with.

The baby sat up. His eyes focusing on each in turn. Like an augur bit, Joe said, cut right to the core. He and his partner left the baby all the gold they had. And their beans and their coffee.

A few days later another prospector caught up with them. "Watch your ass," he said. "Bandits killed a woman and her baby for their supplies."

"So," Joe said, "we all got to suffer a while longer."

The last letter delivered to the Zion City Post Office was a notice from the Postmaster General. Service was to be discontinued as of January 1, 1930, the Fortieth Anniversary of the Founding. The state took Zion City off the Arizona Road Map.

Salem, Zion.

Salem, Odile. The night she died, I dreamed I wore one shoe. To dream of shoes means loss by theft, or act of God.

Joe and Cumi and I stood a long time by her grave, not wanting to close it. For twenty-five years Odile had been in my sight more hours of the day than not.

"I named Cumi," Joe said, "after the words Jesus used to call that dead little girl. *Talitha cumi!* Damsel arise! And up she sat. Arise! Just like that." We both looked down at Odile, but we didn't say a word.

The night Joe got sick, I dreamed I saw an open window. An open window means a friend of twenty years will leave you. I got up and went into Joe's room. He wasn't breathing. "*Cumi*, Joe," I said. "*Cumi*." Joe sat up and took in air, looking right past me.

"I'm late," he said, putting on his pants. "Thank you, Ma'am, for supper." He kissed me at the door and rode away on Cumi.

"Salem!" I called after Joe, risen to a new life.

Then it was very quiet. It seemed to get more quiet every day. It got so a house falling off the mountain made about as much noise as a snowball. Sometimes, for no reason, I'd get dizzy. I was up watering the cemetery when I got so dizzy I fell down and couldn't move. I lay there with my ear pressed to the grass and my feet hanging over the valley, wondering if a city on a mountain was such a good idea. After that, when I got dizzy, I went back to the house as fast as I could. I always made it, though once I spent a long while lying half in the doorway. One night I was lying face down on the floor, hoping that I'd be able to get up soon and fix my supper, when a pair of red shoes walked in the door. I could imagine what kind of noise the high heels should be making on the wooden floor, but the shoes' advance was soundless. I rolled onto my back. On top of the shoes was Madeleine. She bent over me, and I saw her lips say, "How do you feel?"

"I feel," I said, "water going down the drain."

She sat on the floor and talked. I heard some of it, not much. She kept turning to face the past. She had been on the stage or someone had. Her daughter? Her lover? She woke up to see someone in her room. Nils? Claude? Her husband or husbands had died suddenly, drank, took too long too die. Sometimes I thought she knew I couldn't hear her and was saying anything that came into her head. Once she wept, and twice she laughed suddenly.

When I could get up, Madeleine unpacked a bottle of wine—from California. She poured me a glass, leaning close. "Ruthie," she said, "come down to the valley with me."

"What?" I said, pretending not to hear her. She shook her head.

"I worry about you, Pearl dear," she said raising her glass. "I dreamed I saw you holding an orange."

I laughed. "At my age," I said, "it had to be the seedless kind."
Madeleine sat during the day in her old house, though the
roof was gone. She set out lunch on the floor, and every day was a
picnic. Twice more she asked me to go down with her. Twice
more I didn't answer. Then one day after lunch, I fell over on
Seraphim Street and didn't stop rolling until I hit the front of the
post office. Madeleine dragged me back to the house. She held
my head in her lap—trying to convince me the planet wasn't
spinning.

"Please, Ruthie," she said, "what am I to do? Come down with
me." For a minute I almost thought she was Eli.

"You know I can't," I said. "You always knew, Madeleine."

She shrugged. "You're right," she said. "How unchanging you
are." She put my head down on the floor and went to the stove. I
closed my eyes. She came back. ". . . hot," she said and poured
something into my ear. It felt like lava, but it was cooking oil.
Madeleine took a hair pin and pulled from my ear a cone of wax
as long as a toe, as hard as amber. She did the other ear. Her breathing sounded like an avalanche, like a house falling.

I sat up. "Did you know," I whispered, "you could cure me all
along?"

She shrugged again, a very French shrug, a smile and roll of
her head. "Of course," she said.

She kissed me at the door. "Oh, Pearl," she said. "In my
dreams the earth is flat."

Madeleine's leaving sounded louder to me than the whole
Desertion.

That night I dreamed I was awake. A person who dreams of
waking has lived too long.

Now, after all this, the messenger has come.

I lit the Sabbath candles in the windows. In the valley down
below, the gas wells burned like camp fires. I lit the lamp on the

table too and sat down to read my messages. In the big envelope was an artist's study of a statue of Father. He was reclining on a marble base with his right hand raised to Heaven. One hundred feet from toe to halo—bronze. A letter from Brother Johanson, Shepherd to the Lamb of God, described the statue as The Tomb of the Prophet. They wanted Father's body and mine, if I was willing—but not Mother's. It hurt. Even me, it hurt.

I pushed the Shepherd's message across the table into the darkness. What the eye can't see, Mother said, the heart can't remember. Then I opened the other letter.

It was from Eli. Eli, who was a hundred if he was a day. I recognized the large awkward writing, almost as halting as his speech. *Dear Ruthie,* he wrote, *Are you still alive?* There was a picture too, a snapshot of children standing beside a pool of water as blue as any sky. Eli was invisible behind the camera, but there were rows of pink faces, eyes squinting into the sun. Father's eyebrows. Ma's white teeth. One bland round face in the back row. Better watch that one, I wanted to say. *Dear Aunt Ruth. Dear Great-Aunt Ruth. Dear Great-Great-Aunt Ruth.* Looking at that picture I felt multiplied. Immortal, almost.

Yet invisible. The night wind blew in my doorless door and out my curtainless windows, and I had nothing to hide, and no one to hide it from. Except a messenger from Oregon—from Hell, maybe. But what did a life alone in the desert, lighting candles and hiding bodies, have to do with Father's vision of the city on a hill filled with divine light and brethren, or at least sheep? It was a puzzlement. It made my head ache. I filled the tub from the reservoir on the stove for my Sabbath bath. Sitting in the water with my knees tucked up under my chin, my body looked like a shank of old rope. It shocked me after those rows of soft pink faces. I'm so dried up, I thought, that if I stayed in this tub until the crack of doom I wouldn't soak up as much water as a rock. I sat a while, trying to will my pores open, then I heard footsteps behind me.

Four-footed footsteps. It was a lamb, with just a little red dust in the whitest of wool. I got out and reached for my nightgown, but the lamb knelt and began to lick my toes. To chase drops of water up my leg. Each spot he licked took on the moist pinkness of his tongue. I sat down. His breath was hot. He licked my hands, my shoulders. He went in circles around each breast and left it round and young. He licked my stomach and my thighs. I was warm and swimming in warmth. I curled in the chair as if it were my mother. The lamb kissed me on the forehead. Put his hands on my head. Kissed me on the lips. I floated.

I dreamed I was riding a bicycle up the Champs Élysées. It was the Tour de France, and crowds lined the way. All the women in the race were pedaling like fiends, their ball dresses blowing back into their faces. Oh, how the tulle itched, but we were young and strong, and one of us was going to win. Madeleine or Mother or Odile or the girl who looked like Eli or me. We flew through the Arc de Triomphe. The crowd went crazy.

I woke up with the sun warming my toes. The candles had burned to stumps in the windows. I dreaded moving, but when I sat up I wasn't sore. I stood and pulled on my nightgown. Then I danced across the floor. The hollow sound of my footsteps stopped me. I heard it as I had the night Madeleine restored my hearing. It terrified me. Only a person who wanted to die could hear it and not think so. A person who had prayed for years that God would fold this house in his arms and take it down the mountain. Prayed to die. I backed across the room, almost too scared to move, and bumped into the sideboard. A dish hit the floor and shattered. I grabbed at something falling and caught a stick of dynamite. A person tired of living and of praying might be tempted, after a while, to help God gather up this house. I had taken two sticks from a box in the Divine Will General Store. The one in my hand was sticky, covered with little drops like sap on a milkweed. It was probably as old as the dynamite that killed Father, and it occurred to me as I held it that it might not be altogether safe. I picked up the other stick. I thought about the water in the tub, but I wasn't sure that dynamite could be put out as easily as fire. So I walked to the window and threw the first stick out. Threw it as hard as I could and after a breath there was a *boof!* down in the valley, and a little column of red dust drifted up. I threw the other stick.

Boof! I was just bringing my hand down to wipe it when the floor tilted. I headed for the door, but the house disappeared, and I flew up on the wings of a great explosion. I raised my arms and wondered if Father had been pointing at Heaven or trying to grab hold of it. The red face of the mountain came up to meet me. I hugged it as a sheet of flame passed over me, and then I knew I had either blown open a gas well or a door to Hell. I scrambled for a foothold. For an eighty-five-year-old woman who'd thought she wanted to die, I scrambled amazingly well. But the mountain came apart as I touched it. I swallowed sand. It was like trying to climb out of an hourglass. A hand grabbed mine and pulled me up onto Perpetual Crier Street. Then the street too fell away, and the messenger was scrambling beside me. I got a knee on solid ground and pulled him after me. We sprawled on Mother's grave. The ground hummed, was as clear as ice. Looking down I could see Mother and Father, side by side in the earth. Because that was the secret—they were both in Mother's grave. Both looking just the same as the day they were buried, except Father's beard had grown long and wrapped around Mother like a white blanket, and Mother's hair, grown long too, lay beneath their heads like a pillow.

The messenger pulled me to my feet. He was naked except for one white sock. Looking down I saw I was naked too. My body was amazingly soft and pink. But even naked the messenger was white, whiter than wool, and his eyes were as blue as tears, as flames.

He put his arms around me. Under our feet, Father's hand opened, and I saw the hundred-dollar Prophecy, warm and worn in his palm: BORN. A SON.

"This is crazy," I said, shaking, laughing.

"It always has been," the messenger said holding me.

And I remembered Sarah, who was ninety-one when she laughed in her tent and ninety-two when she bore Isaac.

We lay together in the grass as Madeleine had long ago told me men and women did. And in the sky above us biplanes and monoplanes circled. Singing: GLORY! GLORY! or maybe A BOY! A BOY!

"How is it possible," I asked, "for me to bear a child?" The messenger's smile was like lightning.

"All things are possible," he said. He laid his hands on the mountain and dust rained down from the sky, poured up from the valley, until the mountain was healed. Zion City rose from its side like a pop-up village in a children's book. White houses, green vines. Light streaming out every window.

"All things," he said.

And down below I saw my brother Eli, old as Methuselah, waiting in the doorway of my house.

A HISTORY OF INDIANA

All his life, Lancelot Walker would remember the plague of squirrels.

At that time New Hope had existed for just thirteen months. The whole first year no one knew anything, and that was painful. No one knew when to trust the thawed earth enough to plant. No one knew when the frost would come again. That year there were three families and Walker, their bachelor. Even so they couldn't agree on anything. Walker wanted to name the settlement Camelot. He didn't see any harm in it.

"Camelot, Mother of Harlots," declared Mrs. McLintock, the matriarch of the two Georgia families. Mr. Bingham, who was English, thought it smacked of monarchy. "Too much history," he said, "it doesn't seem American."

So New Hope it was, though Walker thought it a melancholy choice. It implied a trail of blasted hopes behind them, and even if that was true, he didn't see why they had to make it official.

That first spring they couldn't even agree what to plant. Walker and the two Georgia families were for corn, but Bingham wanted to plant wheat and hedge with potatoes. "Well, think of Rome," Walker said, trying to lend a little perspective to their troubles. "Do you think Romulus and Remus knew right off what to do?" It seemed to Walker they probably had less to go on, if they were raised by wolves.

"I suppose you think they planted corn," Mr. Bingham said.

"Well, I'm sure as hell they didn't plant potatoes," Walker said.

"Rome," Mrs. McLintock said, "is the Seven-Headed Beast that was and is not but will be."

They planted. The corn and wheat grew. The potatoes rotted.

Walker spent the first January snowed in his cabin, making up a list of names for plants people had spent the summer calling things like *pricky bush* and *big bud*. He went through Livy and Mallory—*Brutus Blade, Cleopatra's Tears, Excaliber Leaf*. He didn't mean to lose the next time.

By the second March things began to repeat themselves, and life seemed on the edge of predictability. The snow melted on time. The ground warmed up, and everyone planned on planting both corn and wheat. Three Welsh families came straggling over the creek and cleared land. That doubled the population, and the whole of New Hope had Mrs. Bingham's second annual piano concert to look forward to. None of the new families had been at the first concert, of course, but they realized what it meant on the frontier to take part in a second annual anything.

It was at the second annual concert that Lancelot Walker met Gwen Llewellyn for the first time.

"Guinevere," Walker said, taking her hand.

"She's just a plain Gwen, Mr. Walker," her father corrected as his daughter became the first person in New Hope to have her hand kissed in greeting. But Gwen had never heard of Arthur's queen and didn't know she was in danger of history. She paid more attention to the piano, which rose from clawed feet to a music stand carved into two griffins—rampant. She had never seen one before.

Walker was sorry she wasn't looking at him but respected her for her love of music. The first concert had been his doing. He was at the Binghams' one morning arguing corn versus wheat and staring at the only musical instrument in New Hope when something rose up in him. He pushed past Bingham and into the kitchen where Mrs. Bingham was boiling porridge.

"Spring awaits you, Persephone. Rise up and play for us!" he cried out to her.

Mrs. Bingham put her spoon down, wiped her hands on her apron. "All right, Mr. Walker," she said. "Since you put it that way."

Mr. Bingham had to put up with cold porridge while his wife rehearsed, but now, in the second year, he was inclined to see it as a sacrifice for the greater good.

"Karl Ditters von Dittersdorf," Mrs. Bingham said and seated herself at the piano in a thunderstorm of purple silk.

"Alas, that once great city," Mrs. McLintock whispered to her daughter, "that was clothed in purple."

The music started.

Gwen's father always said of his daughter, "That one's closed tight as a fist." But at the instant Mrs. Bingham struck the first chord, Gwen looked at Walker and caught him looking at her. She took the music as a gift from him. He smiled, and she smiled back.

When Mrs. Bingham had played every note she knew, repeated exactly the previous year's performance, the concert was over. New Hope clapped and rose, stretching. It was then that Walker heard a sound like something hitting the roof.

"Is that hail?" someone asked. Mr. Bingham opened the door.

The fence, the yard, every tree and stump was covered with squirrels. Walker went out. Squirrels were running across the roof and did sound like hail. They chased each other in circles in the yard like leaves might in a storm. But mostly they looked and sounded like squirrels, hundreds and hundreds of squirrels. Squirrels chewing on the rails and shingles and the bark of the trees. Squirrels as far as anyone could see.

"The wheat!" Mr. Bingham ran by with an ax. When the first dead squirrel came flying out of his grain bin, they all broke and ran—"The corn cribs!" There was much nailing of boards across cracks before each family went to bed under its own roof of squirrels.

The squirrels were still there in the morning. Still there the next day. They ate the swelling buds off the trees. Walker couldn't get over how strange it was no one had seen the squirrels' arrival. "Where do you think they came from?" he asked Bingham.

"Better to ask where we should go," he said, and everyone shook their heads. There was no point in planting corn or wheat if the squirrels would eat it as soon as it came up, and, if they waited much longer, it would be too late to clear land and plant somewhere else—in New New Hope.

"The Lord Jehovah smote the Philistines," Mrs. McLintock said, "with a plague of hemorrhoids."

The next day it rained, but the wet squirrels still sat and chewed. Everyone's roof leaked.

"What we need is some information," Walker said as they all sat in front of the McLintock fireplace. "I mean how often do the squirrels come? Not every year—we know that. But every other year? Every hundred years?"

"How about how long do they stay?" Mr. Llewellyn put in.

"Or how to kill them?" said Mrs. McLintock.

"More like, should we head north or west?" said Bingham.

Walker stood up. "Indians," he said, "are the ones who'd know."

"There aren't any Indians here," Bingham said, and, for the first time, this seemed a bad omen not a good one. What if the Indians knew better? Or had all starved?

"In Lewis and Clark's journal," Walker said, "there's report of a tribe of Indians on the Ohio descended from a Welsh prince named Madoc. I met a trader on the way out here who'd heard about them and said damned if he didn't have half a mind to go see."

"White Indians?" Bingham said. "Welsh Indians?"

Llewellyn shrugged—he'd gotten here.

"I'm going east to find out about these squirrels," Walker said. Everyone looked east. "But I need someone who speaks Welsh." Llewellyn stopped looking east.

"I'll go," Gwen said.

"A woman might be less threatening," Bingham agreed.

Walker shook Llewellyn's hand. "Think of your daughter," he said, "as the Joan of Arc of New Hope."

They left the next morning. The first day every tree they passed was top to bottom with squirrels. The second day they could still hear squirrels moving from branch to branch. But the third day the forest was quiet and empty. The fourth day they came to the Ohio. They went upstream until they found a ford and waded across. On the other side, they sat and put their boots on. The bank was steep and seemed to have been reinforced with cut logs. Smoke rose from a fire they couldn't see. After a while, a woman came to the top of the bank and threw off some trash.

"Hey!" Walker said. The woman shrugged. They sat a while longer, and four men appeared and began to pick their way down to the river. One sat on a boulder about twenty feet off, and three came on. Then another sat down, and another, until finally the oldest man sat down so close his knees touched Gwen's. The Chief had straight dark hair a little longer than Gwen's. Walker thought he saw a resemblance.

"Okay," Walker said, nodding to Gwen.

"'r wiwerod," Gwen said, wrinkling her face and bringing her hands up like paws. Walker heard one more distinct wiwerod and then the Welsh really started to fly. Gwen kept up the pantomime as well, adding a bushy tail to her squirrel. She held out an open hand, let one finger rise from it like growing corn—before her other-hand-as-squirrel nibbled the finger back down to the ground. Gwen's sentences started to go up at the end, and Walker guessed she'd gotten past facts into questions. She pointed east. She pointed west. She shrugged. The Chief started to talk. He pointed at them. He pointed at himself. He tapped his nose twice. The Chief's face was blank—but then he was an Indian. Gwen's face was too, but no more than usual.

"Well?" Walker said.

"I can't understand him," she said, "and I don't think he understands me either." They all looked at each other. Then the Chief turned around and yelled to the man behind him, who passed it on, and another man came down from the invisible village—the trader Walker had met.

"How the hell are you?" the trader asked, sitting down next to the Chief.

Walker told him about the squirrels.

"Well, damn," he said.

"He doesn't seem," Walker said, nodding toward the Chief, "to speak Welsh."

"Well, Goddamn."

"How do you talk to them?"

"I parlay French—all the Indians on the Ohio speak a little of that. You want I should talk to him?"

"Please."

"*Les écureuils,*" the trader started, wrinkling his face at the Chief in his own squirrel imitation. The trader turned back to Walker. "What do you want to ask?"

"Where the squirrels came from and how we can get them to go back there."

The trader asked.

The Chief answered.

"Well, damn," the trader said. "He says that you're asking the wrong questions."

"Damn yourself," Walker said.

"Ask him," Gwen said, "to tell us what he knows about the squirrels."

The Chief swam his hand through the air as he answered.

"He says," the trader translated, "that they're fish." The Chief drew a wavy line in the dirt with his finger. "And fish swim in a river."

"What's that supposed to mean?" said Walker.

"Well," said the trader, "sometimes I don't understand them myself. It could be I'm getting all the words but not what they mean—I mean, would the Chief here get what I meant if I told him I was washed in the blood of the Lamb? But then again," the trader shrugged, "he could be just jerking you around."

The Chief stood up. He took Gwen by the shoulders and kissed her firmly on each cheek—as if she were Joan of Arc. Then he left, his men following.

"Well, Hell," the trader said, leaving too. "Don't do anything I wouldn't do."

They recrossed the river. "Fish," Walker said.

"Fish," he said again when they stopped for the night and put his head in his hands. "Fi . . ." he started, but Gwen stopped him. "Don't say it," she said and, taking off her dress, made a gift of herself.

"Can I talk to your father?" Walker said to her later. "You do know I want to marry you, don't you?"

Gwen rolled over. "You're asking the wrong questions again."

In the morning they began to see squirrels passing in groups overhead. The next day the trees were full of them. One squirrel to a square foot of bark, Walker figured.

"Swim," Gwen yelled at them, flapping her arms. Two panicked squirrels ran forward and fought for a place on the next tree, their place in the rear taken in an instant.

Walker kicked a tree, "Swim." A half-dozen squirrels ran forward, and a half-dozen behind them moved up. "Sshh," he said, and they stood quiet. Even without prompting, every few minutes some squirrels changed trees—always moving forward—toward New Hope.

"Stay here," Walker said, and went off the path. After about fifty feet, the squirrels thinned out; after sixty, the trees were empty. He came back. "They're going somewhere," he said.

"To New Hope."

"Maybe."

When they reached New Hope, there was no smoke coming from the Llewellyns'. Standing outside Walker could tell the place was empty, but Gwen went in anyway, closing the door behind her. The other chimneys were still smoking so Walker knew everyone hadn't cleared out yet. He went through New Hope to the woods on the other side. The trees were full of squirrels—still moving west.

When he got to his cabin, he saw Gwen out planting his corn. She straightened up and handed him the sack. By the time New Hope realized they were back, he had a half-sack of seed corn in the ground.

They all stood dumb watching him plant. The squirrels watching too. "What's this?" Bingham asked when Walker got to the end of the field.

Walker put down the sack of corn. "These squirrels are headed somewhere, and I intend to follow them until I find out. But first I'm going to get in my early corn."

"A time to plant," Mrs. McLintock said. She nodded at the squirrels, "and a time to pluck."

Walker put in another half-sack—as if an extra ten pounds would hold New Hope until he got back. It was almost dark when he left his cabin.

"Da left the family Bible for me," Gwen said. She held a large book against her chest.

Walker took her arm, which was as thin and hard as a tree branch. "He knew you might need it," he said.

"Go on," she said, shaking her head, shaking her arm free. Walker started toward the woods. Looking back, he saw her standing with the book open in front of her, though it was too dark to read. "That which is far off," she called, "and exceedingly deep, who can find it out?"

They all sat watching Walker's field. They were in agreement now. If the first shoot came up and got eaten, they would leave. The day after Walker left, three trappers drifted in and started banging away at the squirrels.

"How much do you get for a squirrel fur?" Bingham asked them when they'd made a big pile in the middle of town.

"Nothing," one of them said, and spit. "We're gonna jerk 'em." Which Mrs. Bingham explained to her husband meant dry the meat for winter. But when the trappers slit the squirrels their knives hit bone right under the skin. There was no meat on them and their stomachs were full of splinters. The trappers shot a few more, out of habit, then gave it up and sat with everyone else watching Walker's invisible corn.

After six days, there was still no sign of Walker or his corn. The grass on the edge of the field was starting to sprout and each blade seemed to come up under a squirrel. Mrs. McLintock shook her head. "I have lived an alien in a strange land," she said.

"So we have," Bingham said.

"Me and mine will be leaving," Mrs. McLintock said, "at sunup." Then Bingham thought Walker had been right about the town's name—How sad to leave New Hope behind with old. The trappers spent the day digging lead shot out of the dead squirrels. Then two of them headed west. Maybe they'd run into Walker or find out what had become of him and maybe not. At any rate west was the direction they always went—west and further west.

"Head north," the trapper who stayed behind advised Mrs. McLintock, while whispering in her daughter's ear, "Come west." Everyone except Gwen spent the night packing. But the Llewellyns hadn't left Gwen anything that needed packing, so no one could tell if she was going to leave or stay.

It was the quiet that woke everyone up. When Bingham opened his door and saw no squirrels, it was almost as much of a shock as seeing the squirrels the first time. The roof was empty, the fences, the trees. An hour later, Walker came home. He went right to his field, stood looking at it until everyone in New Hope was there. Then he told them what had happened. It was a story he only told once, but everyone remembered it. Years later a New Hoper working for the Indianapolis *Free Democrat Locomotive* would write his own version and put the story into history.

The reports coming to us recently from Chicago of the sightings of strange airships should not be taken by the public as a thing altogether without precedence. A certain respected citizen of New Hope—well known in the state as a honest, nondrinking man—thirty years ago saw such a sight right here in Indiana. "The vessel was thirty feet in length," he reported, "and shaped like a bread pan with a loaf risen in it—all the color of new tin. Near the vessel was the most beautiful being I ever beheld. She was rather oversize, but of the most exquisite form and with eyes of sapphire and features such as would put shame to the statues of the ancient Greeks. She was dressed in nature's garb and her golden hair, wavy and glossy, hung to her waist, unconfined excepting by a band of glistening jewels that bound it back from her forehead. The jewels threw out rays of light as she moved her head. She was plucking little flowers that were just blossoming from the sod with exclamations of delight in a language I could not understand. Her voice was like low, silvery bells, and her laughter rang out like chimes. In one hand she carried a fan of curious design that she fanned herself vigorously with, though to me the air was not warm, and I wore an overcoat. On the far side of the vessel stood a man of lesser proportions, though of majestic countenance. He also was fanning himself with a curious fan as if the heat oppressed him.

"Was this," I wondered, "Adam and Eve come to earth again?"

The newspaper reporter didn't mention the squirrels, years later maybe they didn't seem important. But squirrels there certainly were as Walker made his way west. He had to tie his hat on to protect himself from squirrels who, missing a particularly inspired forward leap, fell to the ground like two-pound hail. On the second day he began to hear a sound, a single high note that seemed to shift from one ear to the other. He shook his head. The squirrels around him shook theirs. The third day he came out of the woods on the edge of large clearing. The squirrels were so thick on the ground that he couldn't move without stepping on them. Walker was afraid they might panic suddenly when he got into the clearing. A thousand squirrels would run up the tallest thing in sight—him. So he cut a branch and moved forward, sweeping a dozen squirrels aside for each step. In the middle of the clearing was the bread pan. And the naked woman. The high-pitched noise was coming from the ship. But the woman opened her mouth and made a sound that wasn't too different from the one the ship was making. It made his ears itch. Walker, thinking about the Welsh Indians, almost lost heart for the whole business. But he went forward, starting Gwen's squirrel imitation. It helped that there were a thousand thousand squirrels in a circle around him to point to by way of example. He pointed east. He did the finger-as-corn eaten by hand-as-squirrel. He rubbed his stomach, sucked in his cheeks—tried generally to look faced with starvation.

It was then he saw the man. The woman said something, and the man came around from the other side of the ship, making marks on a piece of flat tin. *Nine hundred thousand and one, nine hundred thousand and two . . .* He's counting the squirrels, Walker realized, watching each mark. The woman finished talking to the man and turned back to Walker. She pointed to her ship. She held up three fingers.

"Three what?" Walker asked.

She pointed at the sun, then moved her arm three times in an arc across the sky, her breasts making their own gentle revolutions.

"Three days," Walker said, holding up three of his own fingers in acknowledgment. The woman nodded. The man moved away, marking on his tin again. The woman watched him for a moment, then shook her head, and something in the way she did it made Walker think, "She's his mother."

The woman looked back at Walker and smiled. She took him by the wrist—her hand was hot. She pointed at him, touched her own chest, pointed at the ship, pointed up. Walker threw his head back and looked at the sky, blue and endless overhead. He felt he was at the bottom of a deep clear well. His lungs ached. He wanted to swim up, burst into what was beyond, into air he had been waiting all his life to breathe. The woman was looking up too. Her fingers burned on his wrist. Against the blue of the sky, her face was white as milk—inhuman. Walker wondered if he knew her name and spoke it, would she disappear with a puff of smoke and a scream like Morgan le Fay? She looked down, and her face was flushed. She looked lonely. Walker shook his head. He took her hand from his wrist and touched it to his lips. It was like kissing a stove. She blushed—red spreading from the roots of her hair to her breasts and maybe lower, though Walker didn't look.

He could feel her watching him as he swept his way out of the clearing. The squirrels stood on their hind legs, and it struck Walker that they looked like little humans wearing fur suits. When he looked back from the edge of the woods, the afternoon sun gave them fur halos. For three days the trees he passed were more full of squirrels than ever. The third night he slept as trees groaned with squirrels. He woke up to absolute quiet.

"They're really gone then," Bingham said.

Walker nodded.

"They was angels," Mrs. McLintock said. "Unfallen creations of God like Adam and Eve, walking naked and not ashamed."

"Well," Walker said, "maybe."

"And they're in Heaven now," she said. "Oh, behold! I heard the voice of many angels round about the throne and the beasts and the elders: and the number of them was ten thousand times ten thousand, and thousands of thousands."

"Angels," Bingham asked, "or squirrels?"

"But why," Mrs. Bingham asked, "didn't you go with her?"

"Because Gwen's agreed to marry me," Walker said. Gwen shook her head, but let Walker take her hand.

"Because you had corn in the ground, you mean," Bingham said.

Mrs. Bingham sighed, as if she saw years of cooked porridge and concerts clearly before her.

Then Walker heard a scratching sound. Everyone else heard it too. On a tree beside his cabin was a squirrel. There was no mistaking that. But it was completely white—an albino. The trapper drew a bead on it with his rifle, eased his finger onto the trigger.

"Don't," Walker said, and knocked the barrel up. The ball went whirring through the high branches. The squirrel didn't flinch. "It's deaf." He stood at the base of the tree. "Swim!" he yelled, "Get!" The squirrel looked like a white X painted on the tree. It hadn't heard its otherworldly summons.

"His head and his hairs were white like wool," Mrs. McLintock cried out, "as white as snow! And his feet like unto fine brass, as if they burned in a furnace! And out of his mouth went a sharp two-edged sword! And when I saw him—I FELL DOWN AT HIS FEET AS DEAD!" She went over like a tree. "Thank You, Jesus!" she said as her sons carried her inside.

Everyone went home to plant.

Gwen put her arm through Walker's. "You should have let him shoot that squirrel," she said. "It won't bring you luck." Walker shook his head.

The squirrel looked down at him with eyes as blue and empty as the sky.

THE DOGEATER

Man Eats Dog

John Santioc of 1415 Bonaparte was charged Wednesday with the theft of a domestic canine. Mrs. Jackson R. Humphrey, who swore out the complaint, told police that she believed Santioc ate the dog. No date for a hearing has been set.

John saw the article in the *Times-Picayune*. He saw it because P'Tete Paul clipped it out and brought it by. P'Tete Paul not only showed John the clipping, he read it out loud to him, punctuating it with gold-capped grins in the direction of Mrs. Humphrey's Chihuahua kennel. When P'Tete Paul finished his reading, he folded the clipping up tiny and put it in his shoe. He jabbed John's shoulder with a grass-stained finger. "Maybe we'll drink later, OK?" John nodded, and P'Tete Paul went off toward Mrs. Humphrey's. P'Tete Paul had been trying to get John to drink for years. John had a sober reputation, and P'Tete Paul wished to cure him of it.

The next time John saw the article was in the red-tipped fingers of a red-lipped woman John found standing in front of the low iron fence that kept the sidewalk out of John's foot of yard. "Are you John Santioc?" the woman asked, holding the short clipping out beside John, as if for comparison.

"*Yon* Santioc," John said. It always bothered him when people looked at his name and called him something else. John stepped over the little iron gate and went into his house. The woman came through the screen door after him. He had not locked the door. He never locked the door. His wife, Louisa, had always been there to stand guard, and, now that she was not, nothing needed guarding.

The front room was the kitchen. John sat down at a red Formica table, and the woman sat across from him. John's house was a shotgun cottage. The rooms led one into another, without hall or entry way, from front stoop to back. From where she sat the woman could see that the table and two matching chairs were the only furnishings in the house. The rooms folded out of one another, defined only by bare plank floors and plaster walls that supported no pictures.

The woman said she was from the *Times-Picayune*. "My name is Delores LeBlanc," she said.

John opened a can of tuna fish, forked most of it onto one slice of bread and covered it with another. If the woman was from the *Times-Picayune*, then the article was her business and none of his. John began to eat. The woman took a manila folder out of her large canvas purse. She put the clipping into the folder and then laid the folder, open, on the red table.

"You are J-O-H-N," Delores spelled it out, "Santioc?" John, with his mouth full, said nothing. Delores tried again, "Yon Santioc?"

The dim light of John's kitchen shadowed Delores LeBlanc's face, made the paint on her lips the same dried red as the Formica. The woman seemed familiar to John now. He smiled, nodded. "Yes, Yon Santioc," he said. His voice was soft, pleasant. His words did not echo out into the empty rooms like Delores's but stayed in the kitchen where he said them.

Delores smiled. She turned the manila folder around so John could see what was in it. The folder was full of John, articles about

John, copies of reports people had filled out about John, copies of forms John himself had filled out. John had been an easy case for Delores. She had found his name in the *Picayune* morgue because John had once been given a Public Safety Award by the mayor for discovering the renewed presence of yellow fever mosquitoes in City Cemetery No. 1. Once Delores knew that much, she had only to get a copy of his City Employment Record, and all was laid open for her. She knew then that John Santioc had worked for the City of New Orleans Mosquito Control Department for forty-eight years. That he retired in 1970 when the City guessed he was sixty-five. She could figure that if he was sixty-five in 1970, then he had to be seventy-six or so now. Because the W-2 forms in his folder once claimed three dependents, Delores could guess at a wife, a child, a steady life. The file gave his home address in 1923 as 1415 Bonaparte, and 1415 Bonaparte was where they sat now. One fact in her folder gave Delores a question: John's 1922 job application listed the City of St. Louis as his previous employer.

"You're not from New Orleans originally, Mr. Santioc?"

The folder of information that Delores showed to John, so much of it in his own large handwriting, seemed to him to give Delores a right to her questions. John tried to remember what Louisa had told him about where priests got the right to know everything. He remembered only that it was very important for what you said to be understood.

"No," John began, "I come from . . ." He tugged at his lip. It wasn't easy to explain all things clearly.

"St. Louis," Delores suggested, answering for him.

That was different then. "Yes," John said, "I came from St. Louis to New Orleans."

"Ah," Delores smiled, made a small stroking motion with one hand on the Formica. "Do you live here alone, Mr. Santioc?"

John nodded. "Yes."

"Wife? Family?"

John wanted to tell the woman important facts for her folder. He wanted to tell her where his Louisa was buried, but he couldn't seem to remember just then. The cemetery was so far out. Metairie? Kenner? Her being dead was such a new and unfamiliar thing. He wanted to tell the woman about his daughter, Celeste, who was an important person. But he did not know where Celeste lived, had not seen her in twenty—no, nearer to thirty years. John shook his head. He could tell the woman nothing of importance.

Delores stroked the tabletop once more. John took a bite of his sandwich. Delores looked first at John and then at the empty kitchen. "Do you eat tuna fish often?" she asked.

"No."

Delores jotted a note and put it in the folder. John put his sandwich down. Actually, he didn't like canned tuna, which didn't seem like fish to him at all. Gloria Latier had given the tuna to him, along with a loaf of bread and a can of beets. Mrs. Latier had been his wife's palm reader.

"People—poor people—poor old people—*elderly*," Delores wrote on the cover of the folder, "Fixed Income—CRIME." She closed the folder and rapped it on the table to get John's attention. "Almost done," she said. Delores made John sit while she pointed a small camera, first at him and then at the empty, high-ceilinged rooms.

"Good-bye, Mr. Santioc," Delores said, opening the screen door. John stood behind her. She turned. "Did you really eat that dog?" Delores believed in surprise.

"Yes."

Delores made a small stroking motion with her right hand in front of John's chest. "Oh," she said, making a note to have some groceries sent up from Renaud's on the corner. "Oh."

The screen door banged shut behind Delores. The hum of its rusty mesh filled the silence the woman left behind in John's house.

John went into the next room, the bedroom, and lay down on the floor. He closed his eyes. He did not open his eyes when the delivery boy from Renaud's beat on the screen door or when the boy called out that he was leaving the boxes by the door. Since Louisa's death, since Mrs. Humphrey's Chihuahua, the old women among John's neighbors had taken to leaving packages of food on his stoop. Gifts, offerings—out of pity or respect, John could not guess.

John opened his eyes later when he heard P'Tete Paul calling to him from the street, but he did not answer him. He closed his eyes again. Not until he was quite sure P'Tete Paul had gone away did John get up and go back into the kitchen. He turned on the bright light that hung over the kitchen table, then went to the cupboard and got out a glass and a tall rectangular bottle. John held the bottle up to the light. A small, white worm floated contentedly in the gold liquid that filled half the bottle. John set the bottle on the table and waited while the worm settled gently to the bottom. Then he poured a little of the gold from the bottle into his glass and took a sip of it. P'Tete Paul had given John this tequila. He had given it to him last Monday afternoon, when John came back so hot, so quiet, in his dark suit from the distant suburban funeral that Celeste's lawyer had arranged for his Louisa. John had never been able to drink. When he would try, standing with the others on the corner by Duval's Bakery, the whiskey or sour red wine always choked him, ran from his throat and his nose onto the sidewalk. John was a great disappointment to P'Tete Paul and the other regulars. They had hoped that John, with his steady paycheck and uncomplaining wife, would take a liking to the liquor and learn to take his turn buying theirs for them. Even Louisa had hoped this sometimes. Louisa had been a good Catholic and often thanked God out loud to her priest that she had such a sober, steady husband. But Louisa had been born in New Orleans, as had all her family anybody would speak about, born where a man is a man most of all when the world or the drink makes him get crazy mean. Louisa once told Gloria Latier that John beat her sometimes though quietly and in places where it did not show. Louisa had lied for the family honor.

The afternoon of Louisa's funeral was the first time John ever tasted tequila. He took a swig without thinking, to please P'Tete Paul. The tequila went down smooth and stayed down easy. P'Tete Paul smiled and went away, leaving the bottle. At first John thought the tequila was good for him because it was so sweet, almost as sweet as the candied grapefruit peels Louisa had made for him sometimes. Later though, after John had tasted more of the tequila, he held the bottle up to the light and realized quite suddenly that the secret of the tequila's goodness lay in its little drowned worm. Its spirit put the whole thing right. Once John had understood such things perfectly; now he felt it coming— pushing—back into him. John smiled then. If the worm was happy, he was happy.

John sipped only a little tequila now. He left his glass on the table and put the bottle back into the cupboard. Then John went through his bedroom into the back room, the parlor, and brought that room's only loose content, a large book, back into the kitchen with him. He laid the book open on the red table. It was a thick book, old and gilded. Its heavy cracked spine allowed it to rest wide open, its pages flat and exposed to light and eye. John put his finger in the book and closed the pages gently on it. He looked at the title, nested in embossed ivy. *The Book of the Fair*, it read in gold, *St. Louis 1904*, in smaller red. John opened the book to the spot his finger held, then rested the same bent finger beside the first paragraph on the page. John did not really read the words on the page, rather he looked at the shape of them and heard Louisa's voice read the words out to him, as she had done many times in the years she spent in John's house. Sometimes even Celeste still heard this voice, these words, in her far uptown house, and not always when she was asleep or unaware.

Filipinos at the Fair

Wild Igorrotes of the Filipino Reservation—The United States has no other wards so little known as the wild Igorrotes, some of whom were shown at the Filipino Reservation at the Fair.

Of these warlike primitives of the mountains and rain forests a great deal has been heard since American interest was directed to the Philippines, but not much was certainly known until the Philippines Commission released its report to the President of the United States prior to bringing the sample Igorrote band to the Fair.

An Igorrote has little capacity for assimilating civilization, and he is one of the natives set down by the Philippines Commission as being not only incapable of self-government, but needing a firm hand to rule him.

Upon his arrival in St. Louis, the Igorrote attracted more attention than all the other primitive peoples at the Fair. Not because of his mysterious reputation was he enabled to achieve this foreign fame, but because he insisted upon eating dogs. Because the Igorrotes eat dogflesh, they aroused the Women's Humane Society to protest, but the Igorrotes insisted that the dogs were a necessary part of their daily and ritual lives, and their regular banquets of dog proved such popular occasions with the visitors that the Fair authorities were disinclined to register protest.

John held the next page, a black-and-white illustration, between his fingers and sighed. The picture showed a small group of naked men standing attentively around a smoking pit fire. Beyond them, a large crowd of men and women in proper finery looked on just as attentively. The caption read:

> *An Expectant Moment*—Igorrotes singeing a dog preparatory to enjoying a bow-wow stew. The City of St. Louis provided these people with twenty dogs a month as their meat ration.

John recognized all the naked people in the picture and one or two of the properly dressed ones. The first time John had seen the black and white photographs, they seemed such inadequate captors of time and place that he failed to realize what the pictures were. Now, after years of looking at them, John's memories had shrunk to fit the photographs' gray shapes. John rubbed the page between his fingers. He knew if he turned the page he would see his grandmother dancing her place in the Dog Dance with the other women. He did not turn the page. He knew that on the page opposite his grandmother he would see a thin-faced Igorrote boy wearing nothing but a breechclout and a Fair guard's hat. The boy was a stranger to him. For years this picture puzzled John. Then one night when she was very pregnant, Louisa caught John staring at the picture of the boy. "Ohla," she said, kissing him on his thin nose. "It will be a boy just like you were." Of course the picture was of him, there had been no other children in the camp, and yet, it was still a stranger.

John closed the book. He should have told the woman where he was truly from, but even now, with time to try and frame the words, he could not put the right sense into them. In the English that was now his only language, all he could have said was, "Igorrote." The word would have had no meaning for the woman. The way it had had no meaning on that day, that bad day, away from the Fair, when the man in the wrinkled green suit had spoken so sharply to him.

John switched off the overhead light, leaned back in his chair.

He had been a favorite at the Fair, not only with the crowds, but also with the guards and the concessionaires. His grandmother had not found much time to watch over him. She was a widow who, in Igorrote fashion, with her husband dead and her age respected, was just coming into her own. So John had been quick to snatch up bits of Western clothes, to mimic the jumpy English words. He was a mascot favored second only to tiny Snow Cloud in the Eskimo camp.

Visitors to the Igorrote camp often gave John small change. His grandmother told him to ask instead for cigarettes, which were better for trade and could always be smoked or chewed. Grandmother had seen little use in money. Most visitors, though, thought John too young for tobacco, and he finally got quite a hoard of small coins. One of the guards at the Fair, Mike, who was always saying John was his boy, offered to take him into the city that was outside the Fair "to spend all them riches." Mike and another guard sneaked John out through the Pyramid of Agriculture. John wanted to buy his grandmother a gift. Now that the nights had begun to cool, she was feeling stiff and unwell. Mike suggested many things to John, pointing vaguely at this shop window or that on their way into the city—it was all strange to John. At the top of a long street far from the Fair, Mike and the other guard entered a shop.

"Wait right here," Mike said. "You'll do just fine." By this Mike meant that John was dressed right, wearing trousers and a buttoned shirt. Mike was right, none of the people who passed paid any attention to him. John was excited. He inched his way down the sidewalk, trying to see into different shop windows. He thought his grandmother would really like a nice dog. A white one, a special one. John was looking at a window filled with a giant white cake that reminded him of the Palace of Manufactures when the hand fell on his shoulder. John turned to find a large man—not Mike—holding on to him. The man said things John did not understand. John tried to talk to the man, who in turn did not understand. At the end of the day John was in a place that was not the Fair, and that was where he stayed.

The man was a truant officer. The place was called the Home for Wayward Children. The people at the home thought John was stupid. They thought perhaps he was Italian. When the first snow came, John caught pneumonia and very nearly died. Later, his favorite teacher, Miss Mallory, would explain to him that what he thought were memories were only hallucinations from when he had been so sick.

It was Miss Mallory who got him his job with the City of St. Louis when he came of age. Miss Mallory's brother was Assistant Director of Public Works, and John was given a job spraying ditches with crude oil to kill mosquito larvae. John liked the job, liked making sure no drainage hole or half-filled tire slipped by unsprayed.

One hot, early morning John found himself working a section with Mike, the guard from the Fair. Mike worked for the city too. He had quit the Fair to take the steadier job. "Eleven years now," Mike said. He told John that he didn't know what had become of the people at the Fair. The Fair had been closed a long time, most of the buildings torn down.

That night Mike took John home for dinner to meet his wife, a soft, kind woman who was bigger around than any woman John had ever seen. When he left, Mike's wife gave John *The Book of the Fair*. "Mike give it me," she said, "but I've not much call for it."

Through the summer and fall John worked for the city. When it began to snow, John took the book and got on a train going south. When the train was as far south as it went, John got off and took a job spraying for mosquitoes. In New Orleans, this was a steady job.

John rose from his chair and carried the book into the bedroom. Even though this room was as empty as the others, to John it had more of Louisa in it. He lay down on the floor.

He met Louisa his first summer in New Orleans. He was spraying in City Cemetery No. 1, coating the stale water that stood in a large funeral urn, and she was etching tiny crosses on Marie Laveau's tomb with a shard of paving brick. Marie Laveau had been New Orleans's greatest voodoo queen. Her tomb was covered with little *xxx*s left by people who still came to "ask on Marie Laveau." Louisa was asking on Marie Laveau particularly hard that day. She was twenty-four and still unmarried. In another seven months she would even be too old for the Holy Comforter Convent that had already taken in her two older sisters. Louisa looked up and saw John; he was wearing his uniform, and it made him look steady. John looked down at Louisa and was strongly reminded of Mike's wife. He felt a rush of unexpected gratitude.

Before Louisa, things had not made sense to John. It was Louisa who explained to him why a woman on Rampart Street who he didn't know would grab his arm or why it made people nervous when he stood under trees at night when the loups-garous might be out. With Louisa's help New Orleans replaced the dimming Igorrote ways.

Now, without Louisa, things were too much trouble to make sense of, like the old women's bundles of food, like the *Picayune* woman's questions. John rested his head on the book and went to sleep.

The next morning a tall pale woman from Sentinel Realty came to see John. Delores LeBlanc sent her, she said. Delores had told the woman, who was an old friend, that John should solve his financial problems by selling his house and moving into one of the new congregate living facilities the city was building for the elderly. When the real estate woman saw the neighborhood, she felt confirmed in her notion of Delores LeBlanc's good sense. The block was already undergoing—the realtor framed the phrase in her mind—"extensive renovation." The smaller cottages had been taken over by young oil engineers, the larger Victorian houses by oil executives. Only a few old people, like John Santioc, or the old crone she'd seen standing across the street by a palm-reading sign, were still holding out. The real estate woman explained all this to John, pointed out the house right next to his as a splendid example of the restoration of castellated Victoriana. John looked over at Mrs. Humphrey's house and nodded. He took the woman's card and shut the door. A good businesswoman, the realtor also left a card with Gloria Latier, the old palmist.

When P'Tete Paul came by that afternoon, John had him carry off the boxes of groceries. "Take them back to Renaud's," he said, knowing full well P'Tete Paul would take them home.

"You want 'nother bottle?" P'Tete Paul asked.

That night, sitting again at his kitchen table, John thought for a long time about selling his house. He had never considered selling it before, although late in the evening of the day he buried Louisa, he had thought about burning it down. After the funeral he came back to the house and wandered from room to room, sipping on P'Tete Paul's tequila. John had gone to several New Orleans funerals with Louisa over the years. She explained to him the hidden purposes behind the color and the noise, but even without her explanations, John felt an instinctive understanding of the mourners' loud and open grief.

The funeral that Celeste's lawyer had arranged for Louisa took place in a quiet, tasteful mortuary that specialized in burying Yankees with no families. Gloria Latier and John were the only mourners. No one else made the long, expensive taxi ride out to the service.

As John paced from room to room that night after Louisa's funeral, he began to collect things, a few things he thought he should put out for the garbage collection: last year's calendar, an empty perfume bottle. John went into the kitchen and got a paper sack. A pile of sewing patterns, a broken string of pearls, a blue stuffed dog, Louisa's bedroom slippers. John kicked off his shoes.

He tore down the large tapestry of the Last Supper, pushed all the saints' medals off the dresser. He took off his coat and his tie and threw the full paper sack out the back door into the yard. He began to clear the parlor in the same way. China, heavy framed pictures—all went out the door and were scattered across the yard. John took off his pants. He began to cry. He got out his ax. The pieces of a small horsehair chair went out the back door. John laid his ax into the sofa. He began to scream. By the time it became too dark to see in the house, John had already finished chopping up the cherry breakfront, the whatnot, the great poster bed—all the things Louisa had bought and polished and cared for. It was then that John thought about setting fire to the walls and floors of the rooms. But he knew he would not. He knew that if Louisa had been with him that night to read it out, *The Book of the Fair* would have told him:

> *Death Followed by House-Wrecking*—The death of an Igorrote is followed by a great clamor in the house. All the members of family set up a great shrieking and crying, and oftentimes the men take out their bolos and hack right and left at the furniture and the belongings of the house.

John knew that he would not burn down his house, knew Igorrotes never destroyed the houses of their dead, because he knew that if in grief the best you could hope for was a house clean of belongings and a mind clear of bad memories, then to succeed at this, the house and the mind had to remain standing.

His house emptied, John had gone quietly, naked, to the City Cemetery No. 1 and, after pouring Marie Laveau a little tequila, slept quietly on her tomb.

John turned out the kitchen light and put the realtor's card in the parlor with *The Book of the Fair*. He lay down on the parlor floor, and, after a while, he fell asleep.

The next morning John saw the article that Delores LeBlanc had written for the *Times-Picayune*. P'Tete Paul did not have to bring a clipping by this time. Delores LeBlanc arranged for John to receive the whole paper. Delores's article was in the *Times-Picayune* Living Section. John had a very hard time understanding it.

The first paragraph was about the number of people receiving Social Security checks.

The next two paragraphs told about an old woman arrested for shoplifting bologna and an old man who ate cat tuna.

The last three paragraphs were mostly about John. The article concluded with a large picture of John biting into his sandwich. The caption read: "Chihuahua Salad Sandwich?"

After reading the article, John poured himself a glass of tequila and drank it all. Today he felt he couldn't wait until dark. John sat staring at the floating worm. He thought about the dream he had had the night of Louisa's funeral. It had come to him as he slept on Marie Laveau's tomb. In his dream he had been staring into a bottle of tequila, just as he was doing now, but instead of a worm floating in the tequila, there had been a tiny, hairless dog. It drifted slowly head over stub tail until its bulging eyes came to rest on John. Then the dog smiled.

John sighed now, got up and put the newspaper in the parlor in *The Book of the Fair*. He looked out his back door toward Mrs. Humphrey's. A round wheezing Chihuahua came to the iron fence and gazed at him sadly. John went back to the kitchen.

When he had awakened from his dream that night on Marie Laveau's tomb, it had been clear to him what he had to do.

He should have bought a dog to exchange for his grandmother's health; that he had not was no fault of his. Since then, though, the fault was all on his side. If he had killed the right dog when Celeste was born, she wouldn't have forgotten her people in that high-toned convent school Louisa sent her to. If he had had the right dog on that first morning when Louisa said she was too tired to get out of bed, then she would be home guarding his house instead of off in a crypt under an Interstate overpass. John understood why the worm's death made for good, and he had no excuse for not understanding what he had to do.

At sunrise he had returned home, gone into his backyard, and beat on Mrs. Humphrey's fence with an arm of the sofa. The dogs ran barking. He grabbed the neck of the first dog that reached the fence and, snapping it firmly, tossed it up and over into his own yard. The fire, over which John first singed and then boiled the dog, he built out of pieces of the mahogany poster bed that had been Louisa's dowry. The mahogany burned bright with beeswax.

After he had picked the dog clean, he gathered up the hot bones and crossing, still naked, to City Cemetery No. 1, laid them on Marie Laveau's grave. He did not ask on Marie Laveau. He wanted only to thank her for his Louisa.

The day Delores LeBlanc's story appeared in the *Times-Picayune* John saw Celeste's car pull up in front of his house. It was afternoon, and he was sitting on his front stoop. The last car of Celeste's John had seen was black and tan with big wings over the trunk, but he assumed this long cream-colored car belonged to Celeste. He remembered his daughter as a person devoted to owning and averse to borrowing.

Celeste did not get out of the car right away. She checked the house number posted by John's door against the address given in the clippings she pulled from her purse. She was pretending not to recognize John's house.

John shook his head. This was the one thing Louisa had explained to him that he never understood. Louisa had arranged for her Celeste to attend school at the one of the finest schools in New Orleans, at the Convent Sacré Cœur, by having Gloria Latier's cousin in Washington, D.C., declare Celeste a foreign national. The letters Louisa paid to have typed and sent to the school introduced Celeste as the illegitimate daughter of the Philippine

Ambassador. Louisa, and Celeste, understood that this was the way of the city—that although New Orleans had a long, grand memory, it was, like any old woman's, not too fixed on the details. It was up to anyone who possibly could to supply his own history, at an advantage, of course. For Celeste it had all worked faultlessly. There might have been, probably still were, people who suspected her of not being all she said, but no one thought to accuse her of being a Filipino pretending to be a Filipino.

John had never understood how Celeste could so easily, so voluntarily, surrender what he himself had been forced to give up. How could she have left her people, her family? Louisa had understood. She had never asked for Celeste, even on her death bed.

Celeste got out of the car and crossed the sidewalk. John opened the little iron gate for her. Its hinges screamed in protest at this unusual exercise. Celeste slapped her leg, and a large dog got out of the car and followed her into the yard. The dog was black and tan, the color of Celeste's old car. She traveled with the Doberman for protection. Celeste and the dog followed John into the house. The Doberman was panting heavily by the time Celeste and John got to the kitchen table. It let out a sigh and sank to the floor by Celeste's chair. Celeste prided herself on being trim for a woman of fifty, but she tended to feed the Doberman whatever food was not allowed on her current diet.

"You have a nice car," John said.

Celeste nodded, paused a moment then nodded more firmly. She opened her purse and dropped her packet of newspaper clippings on the table. "Look," she said, "just what the hell are you trying to do?"

John rubbed a finger across the Formica. He did not look at Celeste. Celeste stopped for a moment, shifted gears. With all the "crazy man" press, she had forgotten what a soft malleable man her father was. She tried to make her voice smooth, like her mother's.

"Please, Father, you don't know what a bad time this is for this kind of publicity. Your youngest granddaughter is to be married next Saturday to a vice president of the Hibernia Commercial Bank—who is also the son of the chairman of the board of the Hibernia Commercial Bank." Celeste felt the emphasis of repetition was necessary. Her father never understood important things.

"Granddaughter?" John asked, looking up at Celeste for the first time.

"Yes, yes," Celeste took another clipping from her purse and gave it to John. It was an engagement announcement, but John didn't read the notice, he only stared at the girl's picture. "My baby, Anna Lynn," Celeste explained, tapping the back of the clipping.

John looked up at Celeste. When Celeste was a baby, John thought she looked like Louisa. Now he could see clearly that if she took after anyone it was after him, after the hollow-eyed, thin-cheeked boy in *The Book of the Fair*. Anna Lynn, though, with her broad nose and round, smiling cheeks really did look like his Louisa. Celeste nodded. She could tell what John was thinking. Celeste personally thought that Anna Lynn took too much after her maternal grandmother and that once she married and was free of Celeste's endless diets, Anna Lynn would very quickly fill out to look exactly like Louisa.

Celeste took a cookie from an open tin on the table and fed it to her Doberman. The realtor friend of Delores LeBlanc's had sent the cookies to John.

John heard a crunching noise and looked down in time to see the Doberman licking crumbs off the floor.

"So you see, Father, if you keep on, it's Anna Lynn who'll suffer. You have to be reasonable."

John wasn't sure he knew what that meant.

"I've arranged with my lawyer about selling this old place, I'd handle it myself, but the wedding . . ." Celeste broke a cookie in half and then dropped both halves on the floor for the Doberman. John watched her carefully. "You need someone to take care of you," she said.

John began to smile. He took two cookies and gave them to the Doberman. He smiled at Celeste. She smiled back at him. It was the perfect clearness of it that made him smile. He had been wrong about Celeste. She understood. Understood not only that he needed someone to care for him, that Louisa's death had ripped a hole in him, she understood the other things too. In the dream Marie Laveau had given him it had seemed that he was the only one who could put things right, make them good again, but now he saw that this wasn't true. Celeste was there, and she understood what needed to be done. She had come to show him the dog she was fattening for Anna Lynn's wedding.

John set the whole tin of cookies on the floor. Crumbs flew across the floor as the Doberman crunched into his treat. Celeste looked from the dog to John, a smile still set on her lips. John smiled back, and still smiling began to cry. He was happy. Everything was going to be done right.

Afterword

Eight of these eleven, including the title story "Underground Women," first appeared in my short story collection *The Dogeater*, which won the 1987 Associated Writing Programs Award in Short Fiction and was published by the University of Missouri Press. "Civil Service" and "A Story Set in Germany" were written at the same time but, though published in magazines, were never in a collection. "Carpathia," which begins the book, is a short short story I wrote for the anthology *Micro Fiction*, which was published in 1996. In one of my life's highpoints, I was at Symphony Space in New York to hear Barbara Feldon read it as part of the Selected Shorts Series. She had played Agent 99 on the TV show *Get Smart*. I was such a big fan as a kid that I sported an Agent 99 haircut for several years.

Micro Fiction was edited by Jerome (Jerry) Stern, one of my first writing teachers. He was the founder of the World's Best Short Short Competition at Florida State University where each year the writer of the best one-page short story won one hundred dollars and a crate of Florida oranges. I dedicated *The Dogeater* to him. Jerry died too young at age fifty-seven in 1996, but I am the writer and teacher I became because of him, so I once more dedicate the stories of *Underground Women* to him. Though I wrote "Carpathia" later for *Micro Fiction*, I had written several short shorts while I was still technically an undergraduate at Florida State. I say *technically* because it took me ten years to get my B.A. I may have set a university record for the number of writing workshops I took over those years, all while I was *technically* a history major. I wrote "Civil Service" for my first writing class at FSU, Janet Burroway's Fiction Technique, which was built around lectures that would become her seminal writing text *Making Fiction*. One day she started reading a student story aloud. Because she had been an actress, she read our work grandly—imagine Dame Judy Dench doing it. I sat listening and thought, *Wow, I wish I could write something like that*. And then, *Wait, that's my story!* Her voice made it sound unrecognizably better. She finished by saying that although she had told us she didn't expect us to be writing *New Yorker* stories, *this* was a *New Yorker* story.

I'm not sure how many students in that sophomore class knew what the *New Yorker* was, but I took what she said literally. I paid to have someone type a clean copy of "Civil Service," the first story I had ever written, then I mailed it to the *New Yorker*. Because I had an investment in the typing, I insured the envelope for twenty-five dollars and requested a signed receipt upon delivery. I waited for months. I sent a query. Someone replied politely on *New Yorker* letterhead that they had no record of the story. I now can imagine a clerk at the *New Yorker* refusing to sign for the delivery of an unsolicited short story. But I took the letter to the post office and collected my twenty-five dollars. So it's true: the first money I earned from writing was for a short story I sent to the *New Yorker*.

It took me ten years to finish my B.A. because I was caring for my parents who were in their forties when I was born and died in their sixties after having been ill for years. Many of these stories reflect their lives more than mine. Wilhelmina, the Women's Army Corps veteran in "Willy," draws on my mother's life, though the funeral in Arlington National Cemetery is based on the funeral of my father, a West Point graduate. The cares of aging, the sense of mortality that fills stories like "A Clean House" with its dying narrator cared for by a young woman who thinks she is a robot and "Tertiary Care" about a widower who moves from a small town to Iowa City to be near the university's hospital reflect the time I spent in my parents' world, filled with trips to the doctor, to the emergency room, stays in the hospital. I wrote those stories soon after my parents died, leaving me free to leave Florida, to move to Iowa City in 1984 to study at the Iowa Writers' Workshop.

These stories were not like the work other students were doing. One of my teachers at Iowa called me "the last living meta-fictionist." *Last living* was certainly not true. Jorge Luis Borges and Donald Barthelme were still very much alive. What he meant was that the days of the ascendency of fiction questioning and playing with its own structure, of a Barthelme story regularly featuring in the *New Yorker* were over. The official language of the workshop was the minimalist, realist style of Raymond Carver with its echoes of Hemingway. There was not much sympathy in my workshops for the surreal or for my use of the historical mixed with the surreal. The other students were so critical in my first Iowa workshop that I left the classroom not knowing if I could trust my ability to chose *and* over *but.* My husband said I shook my head in my sleep, muttering, *No, no.* But I survived. Also, I escaped—that is to say, I graduated with my M.F.A. I wrote "The History of Indiana" and "The History of the Church in America" in a burst of creativity after I finished my last workshop at Iowa but before I graduated. They would be in my thesis, but in the Iowa of those days, no one ever read student theses. I remember feeling giddy with the freedom to write what I wanted.

Stories like those two and "The Dogeater" and "La Mort au Moyen Âge" came from my habit of writing in libraries, hidden away in remote corners. When restless, I would roam the stacks, discovering books like Edward Topsell's *The Historie of Four-Footed Beastes and Serpents* (1658) and Marshall Everett's *The Book of the Fair* (1904) and writing stories around them. "Underground Women" did not come from the library but from cinema which would turn out to be another lifelong source for me, inspiring my poetry collection *Cinema Muto* and the novel *My Life as a Silent Movie*. It was also inspired by a trip to Paris where I did indeed see a dead woman on the floor of a laundromat. "Underground Women" became the seed for my first novel *The Museum of Happiness*, though I moved the story back in time to the Paris of 1929.

Now, with wonderful writers like George Saunders in the world, I think these stories that mix the surreal and the historical fit the current reading moment better than when I wrote them. The collection has long been out of print, but editors kept finding it to include its stories in anthologies and texts. Readers write to me or write blog posts and repost the stories online. My poems, novels, and stories are my children, and so I do not like to have favorites. But I do love these stories in *Underground Women*. It was a joy for me to reread them, something not always true when an author rereads early work. So I am grateful to the University of Wisconsin Press and delighted to have them sent fresh into the world. I hope you, dear reader, enjoy them, too.

Jesse Lee Kercheval
Madison, Wisconsin

Jesse Lee Kercheval was born in France, grew up in Florida, and now divides her time between Madison, Wisconsin, and Montevideo, Uruguay. She is a poet, fiction writer, and memoirist and the author of *The Museum of Happiness* and *Space*, winner of the Alex Award from the American Library Association. Her poetry collection *America that island off the coast of France* won the Dorset Prize and is forthcoming from Tupelo Press. She is also a translator whose translations include *The Invisible Bridge / El puente invisible: Selected Poems of Circe Maia*. She is the Zona Gale Professor of English at the University of Wisconsin–Madison.